AN AMISH BUGGY RIDE

ALSO BY SARAH PRICE

AN AMISH BUGGY RIDE

Sarah Price

Waterfall
PRESS

Published by Waterfall Press, Grand Haven, MI

www.brilliancepublishing.com

Amazon, the Amazon logo, and Waterfall Press are trademarks of Amazon.com, Inc., or its affiliates.

ISBN-13: 9781477826188
ISBN-10: 1477826181

Cover design by Kerri Resnick

Library of Congress Control Number: 2014942339

Printed in the United States of America

To my husband, Marc, for being my knight in shining armor. Where words were once used to hurt, you taught me that it is possible to use them to heal. <3

Master, which is *the great commandment in the law?*

Jesus said unto him, Thou shalt love the Lord thy God with all thy heart, and with all thy soul, and with all thy mind.

This is the first and great commandment.

And the second is *like unto it, Thou shalt love thy neighbour as thyself.*

On these two commandments hang all the law and the prophets.

—Matthew 22:36–40 (King James Version)

A Word About Vocabulary

The Amish speak Pennsylvania Dutch (also called Amish German or Amish Dutch). This is a verbal language with variations in spelling among communities throughout the United States. For example, in some regions, a grandfather is *grossdaadi*, while in other regions he is known as *grossdawdi*. In some books, you might see "thank you" written as *denke* or *denki*, although I've chosen to use *danke* in my books.

In addition, there are words such as "mayhaps," or the use of the words "then" or "now" at the end of sentences, and my favorite expression—"for sure and certain," which are not necessarily from the Pennsylvania Dutch language/dialect but are unique to the Amish.

Also, many Amish speak English in a manner that is grammatically incorrect, such as the following phrases: "Go throw down the ladder some hay," "I wonder that," or "Put the manure on the ground in the barrel." Such expressions are not grammatical errors but authentic dialogue, idiomatic ways of speaking, based upon my firsthand experience growing up in a Mennonite family and living among the Amish in Lancaster County, Pennsylvania.

The Pennsylvania Dutch used in this manuscript is taken from the *Revised Pennsylvania German Dictionary: English to Pennsylvania Dutch* (1991) by C. Richard Beam, Brookshire Publications, Inc., in Lancaster, Pennsylvania.

Please refer to the glossary at the end of the book for definitions of the phrases and words that appear in these pages.

PROLOGUE

Early December 2014

Kate stood at the kitchen window, peering through the frosty glass as huge, ragged snowflakes silently blanketed the driveway. Already, three inches covered the gravel. Most of the other youth had departed already. Only a few still remained, mostly those who lived on neighboring farms: Ella Riehl, John and Samuel Esh, and Hannah Hostetler.

"You need a ride, then?"

Kate turned around, her dark-brown eyes adjusting to the contrasting brighter light of the room. She smiled when she saw Esther standing beside her. Just a few years older than Kate, Esther seemed much more confident. It was a confidence that Kate admired, and she sometimes wished that she could emulate the young woman.

But they were as different as different could be. Esther was tall and willowy with blond hair and hazel eyes that often looked green when she wore darker dresses. Kate, on the other hand, was more petite with brunette hair and dark eyes. She had never quite gotten over her shyness around others, especially the older women in her youth group.

"*Nee*," Kate replied, her black jacket already slung over one shoulder. "*Bruder* David should be here any minute."

Esther nodded, glancing over her shoulder at the simple clock that hung on the wall. Kate's eyes followed. Eight thirty. It was growing late, and with all of that snow, she didn't want any delays getting home. Esther looked as concerned as Kate felt.

"I saw him earlier," Esther said after a moment of hesitation. "Thought he left with Ruth, ain't so? He wasn't singing with us . . ."

With a simple shrug of her shoulders, Kate refused to reply. It wasn't her place to speculate about whom David ran with and even less her place to gossip about whom he might be courting. And if others suspected that David left with Ruth earlier, that was none of her business . . . as long as he returned to take her home.

Esther raised an eyebrow. "I could ask my *daed* to take you home, if you'd like." She glanced over her shoulder at the small group of remaining people. "Or mayhaps one of the Esh brothers could?"

"David will come," Kate replied instead, turning back to the window, silently willing David to appear. *Please don't embarrass me again*, she prayed silently. The last thing she wanted was for Samuel Esh or his younger brother, John, to feel compelled to drive her home in this dreadful weather. "I didn't even know it was to snow at all. Sure am glad we don't live far."

Five minutes passed before she saw the familiar buggy, a pair of black-and-white fuzzy dice hanging from the rearview mirror, pull into the driveway and stop in front of the porch. Relieved, and a touch irritated, she hurried toward the door, pulling on her jacket as she passed the remaining group of young people. Despite recognizing them, she lowered her eyes as she passed. Since they were older than her, she only knew them well enough to lift her hand, a bashful wave good-bye, as she reached the door to leave.

The cold air startled her and she flinched as she stepped through the door and the driving snow hit her face. Blinking, she saw David waiting for her at the bottom of the porch steps and she made her way toward him, shivering. She clutched at the throat of her jacket, making certain that it was closed properly.

"You ready, then?"

Kate reached David's side and looked into his face. He stood before her, his eyes bloodshot and his brown hair tousled, snow-flakes clinging to his curls. Despite the cold weather, he wore neither coat nor hat. She frowned. "Something wrong, David?"

He shook his head, overemphatically. "*Nee, nee,*" he mumbled. "Just get in." With a wild wave of his arm, he gestured toward the buggy. The way he avoided her eyes struck her as odd and, as she began to accompany him to the buggy, she inhaled deeply.

With a frown, she put a hand on his arm to stop him. "Again, David? Really?"

"What?"

She knew that look on his face as well as the tone in his voice: feigned innocence. She didn't buy it for one minute. With a shake of her head, she took a step backward and crossed her arms over her chest. The icy wind picked up, and she was grateful that the wide brim of her black bonnet shielded her face when she tilted her head away from the snow. "I'm not getting in that buggy with you."

"Aww, come on!" He shook his head in frustrated disbelief as he reached for her arm, grabbing it none too gently.

"I'm not going anywhere with you," she hissed in a low voice, yanking her arm free. "Not with you driving, anyway!"

"Well, I'm sure not letting you drive my buggy! It's brand-new and the roads are slick!" he snapped, his temper flaring at the suggestion. Then, trying to look serious and in control, he put his hands on his hips and faced her. "I'm fine, Kate. Just let's go already!"

"You're not fine," she retorted, her voice low and calm. "You're drunk."

"You're not my mother, Kate!"

"Mayhaps you should listen to me for once," she said.

"I did once," he snapped. "And look what happened!"

She cringed at his words, the hateful tone sending her down an all-too-familiar path in her memory. How many times would he say things like this to her? Would he ever tire of making her relive the pain? Each time he found some way to refer to Jacob, that fateful day twelve years ago felt as fresh and vivid as the bright new snow on the ground.

For a long moment they stared at each other, as if the struggle froze them in place at the bottom of the porch steps. Voices from inside came suddenly closer, and Kate realized it was most likely the remaining youth preparing to leave before the storm worsened. Then David looked past her toward the house, his eyes flickering in recognition. Without turning around, Kate knew someone was standing there, observing their exchange.

Pressing his lips together, David leaned forward and whispered, "Come on, Kate!" as he grabbed her arm again and started tugging her toward the buggy.

Whoever was observing them lifted a kerosene lantern high on the porch, and its golden glow spilled onto the driveway. In the light, Kate could clearly see her brother's wild expression. She refused to remove her eyes from David's face. Defiance poured through her veins as she yanked her arm free. "You forsake the Lord, David. *Thine own wickedness shall correct thee.*"

He rolled his eyes and waved his hand at her. "Don't be quoting the Bible to me, Kate."

"You need help!" she hissed.

"The only help I need," he snapped, "is for you to get into the buggy so I can take you and Ruth home! I came back just for you, you know!"

Kate peered over his shoulder at the buggy. Vaguely, she could make out the form of a person sitting on the far side of the front seat. "You have Ruth with you?" She snapped her eyes back to her younger brother, a fierce look on her face. "David Zook!"

"Don't start with me, Kate!" He held up his hand and started backing away from her. "I ain't taken no kneeling vow yet. Neither has she."

Kate sighed. How many times had she heard this from him? Same story, different day. Praying for him wasn't working. Neither were her words. "Well, kneeling vow or not, you are a sinner. And I'm not going to be caught in the presence of a sinner."

He shook his head again.

"In flaming fire taking vengeance on them that know not God, and that obey not the gospel of our Lord Jesus Christ . . ."

"There you go again. You and your Bible quotes." He glared at her. "I have my entire life to know God and obey the gospel as well as the Ordnung! Until then, you either get in the buggy or you walk home, Kate. I'm not fooling with you anymore."

She tilted her chin, trying to ignore the fact that the snow was falling even heavier now. "If those are my choices," she said, "I'll walk."

"Suit yourself." He wasted no time in hurrying back to the buggy and climbing inside. With one final look in her direction, he slid the door shut and, within seconds, the buggy began to roll down the lane toward the road, the horse pulling it through the snow that had already accumulated. She glanced over her shoulder to see if the person who'd brought the lantern to the porch was still there, but all she saw through the snow was the closed front door.

As the buggy disappeared down the road, the blinking lights on the back of it fading away, Kate suddenly felt the consequences of her decision. It was cold. And she was going to have to walk home in the snow. Alone.

On a clear night, it would take only fifteen minutes. Twenty at the most. Shivering, she clutched her jacket tighter around her neck and stepped back onto the porch steps. No one else was around; most of the other youths had already left. The few who remained lived closer; only the Esh brothers would be driving near her parents' farm. Still, it would be too great an inconvenience to ask them to take her home.

Besides, she told herself, the last situation she wanted to be in was one in which she needed to explain David's behavior. *Rumschpringe* or not, she would not lower her own morals and values to accommodate another.

With a big sigh, she lowered her head and began the walk down the lane toward the farm. The snow blinded her, not that she could see much anyway. It didn't matter, though. She knew the way as well as she knew the back of her hand. She had walked these roads for her entire life, all twenty years of it. Straight down the road, left before the hill, and then the first right would take her home.

In her mind, she repeated Bible verses to take her mind off her toes and fingertips. They tingled from the biting wind, so she kept wiggling them. Despite wearing a heavy coat, thick stockings, and woolly mittens, she grew increasingly cold with each footstep. Secretly, she found herself hoping that someone might drive by, perhaps one of the older youths who lingered behind, and offer her a ride. She tried to think of excuses she might make if, or hopefully when, that happened.

But no one appeared.

Turning down the road that led past her *aendi*'s house, Kate's thoughts turned toward David. It made her angry that he scoffed at her for following the Amish religion so closely. Oh, she knew some youths who took the kneeling vow and still kept cell phones. She even heard of a few older people who were on the Internet, using their work computers for pleasure. She just was not one of those types of Amish. When she had taken her kneeling vow the previous autumn, she'd meant it.

And be not conformed to this world: but be ye transformed by the renewing of your mind, that ye may prove what is that good, and acceptable, and perfect, will of God.

That vow was the basis of the Amish religion, after all. Conformity to the world, especially today's world with technology and alcohol, pulled people away from God and away from family. Those harmless cell phones that some of her friends kept tucked deep in their handbags or hidden under their mattresses meant isolation from the community, their family, and, most importantly, God.

The day she took her kneeling vow was the day she threw away her cell phone. Little did she know that David would dig it out of the garbage and reactivate it.

Still, in hindsight, she shouldn't have been surprised. As she'd happily said good-bye to her *rumschpringe*, David eagerly said hello to his.

He was three years her junior and eager for the freedom afforded to sixteen-year-olds in the church. *Rumschpringe.* The time for running around and experimenting with the world and exploring what it had to offer before deciding whether to take the next step: baptism. Most of the youths in their *gmay* only ran around for two years before taking the kneeling vow and committing to the Amish way of life, both culturally and religiously.

Unfortunately, Kate had a sneaking suspicion that David would not follow that path. He seemed to be growing further away from taking his vow, not closer.

As a driving wind blew snow into her eyes, Kate's thoughts turned to Ruth, and how small her huddled figure had looked in David's buggy. With her big brown eyes and freckled nose, Ruth was a pretty young woman. She'd always appeared to be the perfect future Amish wife. She worked hard, spoke softly, and never complained about anything. The fact that Ruth tolerated David's behavior conflicted with the pious nature Kate believed she possessed.

Was it possible that Ruth didn't know?

That thought struck Kate. Was it possible that Ruth didn't smell the whiskey or notice his slurred, aggressive speech? Didn't Ruth wonder why his own sister refused to ride home with him in the buggy that evening? Or did Ruth know and choose to look the other way?

"Dear Lord," Kate whispered. "Please help David see the truth in Your light and free himself from Satan's ways."

As she rounded a bend that began the ascent of the hill just by her parents' farm, Kate quickened her pace. Only a little farther and she'd be home, out of the snow and, hopefully, snuggled in her bed. The second floor of the farmhouse remained cold all winter, but nothing as biting as what she felt now. Once she climbed into her bed underneath all of those quilts, she'd warm up in no time, that was for sure and certain!

The snow started falling even harder. She kept her head bent against it and repeated the Lord's Prayer, mostly to distract herself from her rising anger at David. She was also frustrated with herself for refusing the ride; it was foolhardy to walk alone at night in such a storm. Just as she was about to reach the crest of the hill, she looked up eagerly. She was approaching the border of their neighbor's farm, which meant she was almost home.

Something blinked in the darkness ahead of her. For a moment, she couldn't tell what it was. She had already passed her *aendi's* house and no lights had shone through their windows. Either the storm blocked the glow of kerosene lanterns or they already slept, which would not be surprising since Susan was expecting her first *boppli* in another month or so. She was Maem's youngest sister and had married later than most Amish women. In truth, Kate felt as if Susan were her *schwester* instead of an *aendi*. After all, Susan had lived with them until she'd married Timothy two years ago.

As she neared the crest of the hill, she frowned at the single light that blinked. On. Off. On. Off. *What on earth could it be*, she wondered with more than a little fear building inside of her chest. It looked as if it were located in the field, not the road. That gave her some comfort as she approached. Perhaps the farmer had left a lantern or flashlight in the field?

And then she heard it. A familiar clicking noise. The same noise that buggy lights made at night when they blinked. Yet, buggies had two lights, not one. The unmistakable clicking sound sent a shiver throughout her body. Forcing herself to hurry, she half ran toward the light, her heart pounding and panic coursing through her blood.

The overturned buggy lay in the ditch, only half of the back visible to the eye. The broken shaft, split in two, dangled like a damaged tree limb. The horse was nowhere in sight, having broken free from the lines.

Shaking, Kate placed her hand on the side of the buggy and felt her way toward the door. Her foot slipped on the icy, snow-covered ground, and she caught herself by grabbing the side of the wheel. The whole buggy moved, just slightly, as she steadied herself.

When she got to the door, it was almost impossible to open. The top of the buggy was tilted away from her, leaning down into the ditch, and she couldn't reach the door handle.

"Hello? Who's in there?" she called out, her voice shaking, dread building inside of her chest.

Silence.

Taking a deep breath, she moved toward the front and wiped the snow away from the windshield, peeking inside, afraid of what she would see. At first, she saw nothing. The buggy was empty and she almost breathed a sigh of relief. But as her eyes adjusted to the dimness of its interior, only slightly illuminated from the blue glow of the battery-operated dashboard, she realized that she was mistaken.

Two forms, both dressed in black, lay in a heap at the bottom of the buggy. Without seat belts, they had fallen together and looked almost invisible in the darkness. Kate shook as she reached out a hand to bang on the windshield. "You all right in there?"

Finally, she saw movement and felt a stab of hope as a familiar pair of brown eyes stared up at her.

"Get help, Kate," David managed to say, his voice no more than a hoarse whisper. She thought she saw him trying to reach out to her, but his arm seemed pinned beneath him. She sensed rather than saw him wince in pain. "She's not moving. Go get help."

Frozen in place, she just stared, her heart racing and her mind trying to comprehend what she saw. For what seemed like minutes, she stood there. Was that blood on his face? Why couldn't he move his arm? What was preventing Ruth from moving? Backing away from the broken buggy, she stared at it, the reality dawning on her that David needed help. And fast.

Turning on her heel, she ran the rest of the way up the hill, her feet sliding on the thin layer of ice that lay underneath the fresh, wet snow. She fell not once but twice, managing to scramble back to her feet and continue running on the treacherous road until she came to the lane that led to their farm.

"Daed!"

No one could hear her, but she continued yelling his name as she neared the house. When her feet hit the bottom step of the porch, the door opened; her father stood there in his stocking feet while her mother stared over his shoulder.

"*Wie geht's?*"

Breathless, Kate collapsed against the doorframe, letting her mother's hands pull her inside and pluck at her wraps. "It's David." She stared at her mother first and then her father. She didn't want to say it. What if she had been mistaken? What if it was someone else? Still, whoever it was needed help. "Something's happened. An accident."

"David?"

Kate gulped for air as she nodded her head once.

Her father wasted no time and began to pull on his winter boots and overcoat. "Where?"

"Just down the hill. Toward Susan's house. An accident . . . with the buggy."

With those words, Kate's father ran from the house into the snow. She turned her wide-eyed gaze to her mother and felt the tears start to fall.

"Mayhaps I . . . I best call for help," Maem said softly, the color drained from her face and her voice monotone, as if in a trance. Without reaching for her coat, Maem disappeared outside, undoubtedly to go to the barn where the telephone was kept, since the bishop did not allow telephones in their houses.

Kate stood there, alone in the mudroom, her hands shaking, whether from the cold or fright she did not know. Behind her, in the kitchen, she listened to the loud hissing noise of the propane lamp by the sofa. Glancing over her shoulder, she noticed the unfinished crocheted blanket on the sofa. Maem must have been working on it when Kate interrupted with her shouts for help.

Uncertain what to do, Kate fell to her knees, not caring that she knelt in a puddle of snow. She closed her eyes, clasped her hands together, and then prayed. Her lips remained still as she lifted her heart to God, imploring Him to protect her brother David and Ruth. When she heard the first sirens, she was still on her knees and there she remained until her mother returned with Kate's *aendi*, Susan, both of them covered in snow.

Kate looked up and knew that they both had been to the accident scene. From the way that Maem sobbed into Susan's shoulder, Kate did not need to be told that her prayers had not been answered.

Rising to her feet, Kate followed the two women into the kitchen. Without being asked, Kate began to arrange the furniture for the influx of visitors that were destined to arrive. Surely the bishop and elders would come to pray. Keeping busy was the only way that Kate knew how to avoid facing the reality that tragedy had struck, a tragedy undoubtedly caused by her brother David and his passion for the sour taste of whiskey.

CHAPTER ONE

As she walked along the road toward her parents' farm, she noticed patches of bare earth, an undeniable sign that spring was just around the corner. Along the edge of the road, piles of dirty snow, cleared weeks earlier by the township plows, remained—stubborn reminders of what had been a brutal winter. One of the worst on record, they said.

Now, as the fields began to thaw, flattened brown grass peeked through the remains of the white blanket that had covered it non-stop for the past twelve weeks. The sun was going down and a cold wind picked up. Near the broken split-rail fence, the overturned gray-topped buggy with its broken wheel and wrecked black metal shaft cast an eerie shadow on the exposed ground.

Kate averted her eyes as her path took her closer to the skeletal frame. Every time she took this route, she forced herself to look anywhere but in the direction of the wreckage. She pulled at her black shawl as if trying to ward off both the cold air and the bitter memories of that consequential night.

Had it only been three months ago?

As she neared the damaged buggy, she shut her eyes and counted as dread consumed her. No matter how much time and distance she put between herself and that night, she felt she'd never get over it. *One, two, three* . . . It was the same thing, every Saturday, so she'd learned just how many steps it took to get past the horrible sight. *Twenty-three.* That was the magic number until she would finally pass the spot. *Twenty-three*, just like the number of her favorite Psalms.

Four, five, six . . . While she loved helping her *aendi* with the *boppli*, she hated walking home. Although she could have chosen to walk the long way or cut through the Hostetler's field, she vowed two weeks ago that she wouldn't do that anymore. *Seven, eight, nine* . . . Why hadn't they removed it yet? What were they waiting for? Time seemed as frozen as the ice coating the wheels, trapping the buggy in a pile of snow that the Englische road crew had thoughtlessly plowed up against it. *Ten, eleven* . . .

"Hey, Kate!"

Her concentration broken and the numbers suddenly forgotten, she opened her eyes and turned around at the unexpected sound of her name. To her surprise, she saw Samuel Esh hanging out of the open door of his gray-topped buggy. He waved at her and stopped his horse so that the buggy blocked her view of the damaged fence, the tragic evidence of the accident, and the bitter memory of that awful night.

"Let me give you a ride," he said, a pleasant smile on his face. He tipped back his straw hat, his straight brown hair falling over his forehead until he pushed his bangs out of his blue eyes. Although she did not answer, he moved over on the buggy seat, making room so that she could climb aboard.

Once settled next to him, she stole a quick glance at him, feeling awkward, for she had never ridden alone in a buggy with a young man.

"*Danke*, Samuel," she whispered, folding her hands on her lap and tucking her feet under the seat. She hoped he knew how much she meant it. Her appreciation was for the ride, but even more for his thoughtfulness in offering it. She hoped she wasn't taking him out of his way. From what she could tell, thankfully, his horse had already been traveling in the direction of her parents' farm.

He wasted no time urging the horse to move forward, pulling the buggy farther away from the remnants of the accident. Once they had crossed the crest of the hill, he seemed to relax and slowed down the horse. Holding the reins in one hand, he glanced at her.

"Where you coming from, then?" he asked.

"My *aendi* just had a *boppli*," she answered, her eyes downcast and her hands folded on her lap. She didn't know why, but she always felt so shy and awkward around boys, especially Samuel Esh, who was five years older than she was. Kate knew him a bit through her older brother, Thomas. The two boys had gone to school together, although Samuel was two years older than Thomas. For a short while, during their *rumschpringe* days, Samuel and Thomas had run around with the same youth group.

However, Samuel seemed more worldly and much more knowledgeable than Thomas. That made sense, from what she'd heard of his travels. He'd left Lancaster County four years prior and traveled to New York City, Miami, and Dallas. There had even been whispers that he had stopped at New Orleans for something called Mardi Gras. Kate hadn't asked what that was when Thomas mentioned the topic a few years ago. She only knew from the raised eyebrows and clickings of tongues from the other womenfolk that it was something definitely too worldly for an Amish youth. But no one could complain or reprimand him. After all, Samuel Esh had been on his *rumschpringe* and, at that time, had not yet taken his kneeling vow.

After six months of traveling, Samuel had returned to his parents' farm and settled down to a life of working God's land under His guidance. No one ever mentioned his adventures among the

Englische, although a few members of the *g'may* had seemed mighty surprised when, upon his return, he had immediately started his instructional for baptism.

That was just around the time Kate had turned sixteen, which meant she was finally allowed to attend youth singings and gatherings. She enjoyed that particular freedom and the chance to attend events with her older *bruder*, Thomas. No boy asked to take her home in his buggy after her first social outing. Kate didn't mind. In fact, she was relieved to not have that pressure put onto her young shoulders. She had no idea what she would have talked about with a boy! She wasn't especially talkative, and if she did start a conversation, it was usually with one of her sisters or a female friend, like Verna.

When Thomas began courting a young woman named Linda Schwartz, Kate began walking home from singings with her friends or, if asked, riding home in a crowded buggy driven by a neighbor boy. She hadn't thought much about it, but now that she was twenty, she often wondered what was wrong with her that no one in particular had offered her a ride.

After Thomas had married the previous winter, Kate noticed that most of her friends began courting young men. First she noticed Ella, and then Sylvia, leaving in a different buggy than the one in which they had arrived. When her younger brother, David, began to court Ruth Stoker, Kate was left walking home with Hannah for a few months until she, too, seemed to slip away with a young man to ride in his buggy along the winding roads, leaving Kate alone to walk home from the gatherings.

And then the accident occurred.

"Your *aendi* . . . she lives just at the bottom of the hill, ain't so?" he asked.

Kate nodded.

"Timothy's Susan, *ja?*"

Kate gave a little laugh at the way that Samuel referred to her *aendi*. "*Ja*, Timothy's Susan."

Samuel nodded his head once. "It's a girl, *ja*? Haven't seen Susan at worship with the *boppli* yet."

"The *boppli*'s still small, not even two months," Kate responded.

New mothers tended to keep their newborns away from crowds, especially worship service, until the infants were over two months old. Susan was no different. She fretted about germs, forcing Kate to wash her hands incessantly with special soap that Timothy had purchased at the Smart Shopper. In fact, she had lived in the *grossdaadihaus* when Kate was growing up and had moved out when she wed Timothy two years ago. The newly married couple had moved into a smaller but neighboring farm just down the road from Maem and Daed's property.

Maem had chuckled over Susan's germaphobic condition, commenting to Daed, "Let's see how much of that fretting is left over when she has her third *boppli*!"

It was no secret that Maem and Susan didn't see eye to eye about child rearing. Susan had always been rather critical of the way Maem and Daed let their children have more freedom than most families in the *g'may*. The Zook family was always the last family to pull out shoes from the attic in the autumn. The *kinner* seemed to miss the most school during the plowing and planting season. And David . . . well, *everyone* seemed to have an opinion about David.

"Ruth Ann is her name," Kate added quietly. She still wasn't entirely comfortable with Susan's naming her firstborn after Ruth so soon after the young woman's death.

Samuel remained silent, not speaking for at least a full minute, which felt painfully long to Kate. Finally, he nodded his head and looked at her. "Right *gut* name, don't you think?"

She didn't respond.

When Susan gave birth two months ago, shortly after the New Year, the joyous occasion had brought the Zook family newfound hope and a reason to smile. Kate had been only too happy to volunteer to help her *aendi* on the weekends, giving Susan a little break to rest a spell. It was also a good excuse to visit. Even better, it allowed Kate a reason to escape the heaviness that lingered over her parents' home.

And what a heaviness it was!

How life had changed for everyone since that snowy night in December. She didn't like thinking about it, so she pushed the events deep into the recesses of her brain. She liked to pretend that there was a little box inside of her head, one that allowed her to hide horrible memories. It was a relief to imagine closing the lid, pretending to lock it with an old-fashioned iron key, and hiding it far away in the back corner of her mind. The truth, however, was that the memory of that night and the following days could never remain locked, no matter how many times she envisioned turning that key.

At least she could forget, if only for a few hours, when she was at Susan's. Holding the *boppli* changed everything. She loved holding Ruth Ann, especially when the baby slept. Her small mouth often puckered as if nursing even though she was wrapped in a blanket, all snuggly buggly, with her eyes shut and her tiny chest rising and falling while she napped. A slice of heaven, Kate would think as she gazed at her.

The only downside to helping her *aendi* with Ruth Ann was the inevitable walk home. The first few Saturdays, she walked home the long way, avoiding the place where the buggy accident had occurred. Eventually, she knew that she needed to face her fears and begin walking directly home. She thought it would get easier, but it never did.

Not until today.

The perfection of Samuel's timing impressed her and she said a silent prayer of thanks to God. She still held out hope that the wreckage would be removed soon. It had not been possible thus far. Any attempt would have been hindered by the onslaught of snow and ice that had fixed it in place since the accident in December. So the remains of the buggy still occupied a patch of grass bordering the road, an unwelcome reminder of the past. Technically it was on their neighbor's property. Who knew how long it would remain with so much happening in the *g'may*, a fact that haunted Kate every Saturday when she walked by it.

Today, however, Samuel had saved her that pain with his impromptu stop and invitation to ride the rest of the way home in his buggy.

"Sure will be nice when the snow is all gone, don't you think?"

Kate snapped back to the present and looked at Samuel. His big blue eyes stared at her from beneath the brim of his hat. Despite it still being winter, his skin glowed tan and she knew that he must have started working outside already. The Esh's farm was one of the larger properties in their *g'may*; with eleven children, there was no shortage of labor to work it. Word on the Amish grapevine was that Samuel's devotion to both his family and their farm had been unflagging, especially after he took the kneeling vow.

"*Ja,*" she said, her voice soft. *And then someone can remove that buggy,* she wanted to add but refrained. She had always learned that silence was golden. She certainly did not want to point out the obvious to Samuel Esh or repay his kindness of offering her a ride by complaining.

"Haven't seen you at any singings recently."

She wasn't certain whether that was a question. She glanced at him, surprised to see him watching her with an intensity that made the color rise to her cheeks. Why on earth would Samuel Esh notice if she went to singings? An even better question was, why on earth would he care? After all, he was rumored to be courting Ella Riehl. In fact, many in the community were surprised that their wedding hadn't been announced during the last season.

When she realized that he was waiting for an answer from her, she merely shrugged her shoulders. "Didn't feel much like going, I reckon."

That was an understatement. Between the cold, wintery weather and the dark gloom hanging over her household, the last thing on Kate's mind was attending a singing! Joy didn't seem to be a priority for the Zook family. *Anyone in their right mind could understand that*, she thought.

"I see," he replied, his deep voice low and compassionate. There was a momentary pause as the horse seemed to slow down. Kate glanced at his hands holding the reins and realized that he was doing it on purpose. "And David?"

Kate clenched her teeth and lifted her chin, staring straight ahead. She didn't want to answer any questions about David. Not now, not ever. Rather than respond, she turned her head to stare out the window. It was the Amish way. Rather than reply and say something that might cause regret later, they would merely stop the conversation.

Out of the corner of her eye she saw that he pursed his lips and nodded his head to indicate that he understood her discomfort. She felt relieved to know he would pursue the topic no further.

They rode the rest of the way to her parents' farm in an uncomfortable silence. It hung between them like the oppressive air of a hot, humid summer's night, even though the late-March evening was chilly. She knew what Samuel wanted to ask her. The question was as obvious as sun in the sky. Still, out of respect, he remained silent for the answer was equally clear.

When he stopped the buggy in the driveway, she gave him a soft smile to show her appreciation before she jumped down and hurried toward the house, knowing that if her parents saw Samuel's buggy pulling out of the driveway, they would certainly wonder out loud about how he had happened upon her and what had prompted her to accept a ride with him. Those were questions she didn't want to answer, not tonight anyway.

CHAPTER TWO

The battery-operated clock on her nightstand read 5:05 a.m. It was Monday morning, the beginning of the workweek. Kate lay in bed, staring at the ceiling as she said a silent prayer before collecting her thoughts. It was her morning ritual. Sometimes, in the distance, she would hear the whistle of the train as it approached the station. She knew that if she could hear the whistle, the wind was blowing from the south and it would be a nice day. The previous three days had been delightful, with the temperatures almost hitting the fifties.

Kate favored the mornings, a quiet time of day that permitted her solitude for reflection as she worked in the barn. She loved to be outside when the sun peeked over the horizon, transforming the inky nighttime sky to a pale gray that became a wash of bright colors and ultimately turned radiant blue. Her younger siblings slept in for another hour while Kate dressed in her work clothes and tiptoed past their closed bedroom doors as she headed for the staircase.

"*Gut mariye*, Daed," she said when she saw her father standing by the counter, his back toward her. He stared out the window, one hand holding a coffee cup. As she neared him, she saw that his eyes looked but did not see. Daydreams must have captured his mind. "Daed?"

At the sound of Kate's voice, he shook his head and looked at her. His gray curls remained unbrushed and the whiskers in his beard looked unkempt. The dark circles under his eyes revealed his constant bouts with insomnia. Kate did not need her *maem* to tell her that Daed wasn't sleeping at night, spending the darkest hours of each day tossing and turning, sighing, and, from the privacy of his own room, sometimes crying. The walls of the farmhouse were thin. There was little anyone could do to help ease his pain. What was done could not be undone. That knowledge, more than anything else, surely kept him awake at night.

"Still planning to fertilize the back field today, then?" she asked, trying to smile in the hopes that she could elicit some response—any response—from her father.

Every morning she awoke with one mission in her life: to return joy to her father's eyes. Every night she went to bed knowing that she had, once again, failed. No matter what she did during the day, no matter how hard she worked, there was one thing that she could never do and that was replace David. The realization that nothing she did would ever be good enough for her father left her aching in pain, too aware of the hole in his world, a hole that could never be filled.

He nodded his head. "*Ja, ja,*" he mumbled. "The back field." His tired eyes met hers, lingering just long enough to indicate that his mind was elsewhere. These days, it usually was. With a sigh, he blinked and returned to the present. "Best get started with morning chores, then."

The daily routine established after the accident hadn't changed in months. Daed and Kate spent the predawn hours in the dairy barn, milking cows for a good hour and a half, before the others joined them for their chores. By then, Miriam and Becca would be awake and dressed, hurrying out to the barn to help muck the horse stall and feed the animals.

No one asked questions or complained. Everyone knew what had to be done. Before the accident, Kate had helped Maem in the kitchen while David worked alongside Daed. Now it was Kate's responsibility to help with the manual labor. Gone were her days of baking bread and cleaning house, washing clothes and making beds. Instead, she was destined to spend her early mornings milking cows and mucking stalls, her days plowing fields and spreading manure, and her evenings exhausted from working so hard.

She didn't mind. Not really. It was peaceful working in the barn and the fields. In her younger years, she'd loved the summertime, which brought the chance to stay home from school and work in the fields cutting hay or harvesting corn. She enjoyed being outside, the sun beating on the back of her neck and the dry earth crumbling under her bare feet. The fresh air kept her awake and made her feel alive, and part of her liked it much better than being confined to the four walls of the house.

However, one thing had changed since those earlier years: Daed's eyes no longer sparkled.

She slipped her arms into her work coat before she followed him through the door that led from the mudroom onto the porch. A vision struck her, a memory of his face when she had arrived home that night with news of the accident. His expression, wide eyes so full of fear, would never leave her. It haunted her.

Shaking her head, she pushed the memory away and hurried after him through the morning darkness as he walked toward the barn. The cows greeted them with anxious shuffling, eager for their full udders to be milked. Kate laid her hand on the rump of the nearest cow, a black-and-white Holstein with a crooked tail.

Unlike some of the church districts in Lancaster County, their bishop permitted the *g'may* to use diesel-powered milking machines. It made life much easier, and took less time than hand milking almost three dozen cows. Kate remembered when the old bishop died and a new one was chosen by a lot drawing among the men, one tiny slip of paper fluttering from a Bible that Menno Hostetler selected from the table. His face paled at the realization that, for the rest of his life, he would lead the community, guiding their religious beliefs and cultural assimilation with the world around them.

One of his first acts as bishop was to permit the use of the diesel-powered milking machines. Some of the older farmers quietly rebelled, refusing to switch from the "old ways" to the newfangled technology that many thought belonged only in the domain of the Englische. Kate's father, however, had eagerly jumped on the band-wagon, installing the system as soon as he could. After all, despite having five children, only two were sons. There were not enough hands to milk cows, not if they were to prosper in the twenty-first century.

"Go throw down the ladder some hay," Daed told her, as if she didn't do this every morning.

Obediently, she did as she was told. Climbing the sturdy ladder into the hayloft, she yawned. Like her *daed*, she now suffered from restless nights. That sleep did not come easy to her was yet another change in her life. Still, she never complained. If God wanted her to toss and turn, remembering the events that led up to the accident, who was she to question Him?

By the time the sun crested over the horizon and spilled light into the barn, Miriam and Becca made their entrance. Kate looked up when she heard the door open, the hinge squeaking. As always, Miriam entered the barn first, her chestnut hair perfectly brushed and pinned back, dressed for the day with a work apron covering her clothing. Her soft doe-like eyes always looked so thoughtful and exuded kindness. At thirteen, she was attending her last year of school before she would complete her education at home until she reached the age of sixteen.

Despite the seven-year age difference, Kate and Miriam's similar personalities created a special bond between the two of them. Knowing that Miriam looked up to her, Kate tried to be the perfect role model for her—and for their younger sister, Becca, as well. Miriam responded well, learning from Kate and mirroring her demonstration of humility and righteousness.

Ten-year-old Becca, however, was a different story altogether. Perhaps because she was the youngest and the last child, Becca lacked restraint. This was because she'd been overindulged by her parents, at least that's what Kate suspected.

Childbirth hadn't been an easy road for Kate's parents. She always wondered if they still mourned the loss of their two stillborn babies, sons at that. She remembered all too well the pregnancies and the funerals for the small, lifeless brothers that she'd never had a chance to play with. When Miriam had arrived, the relief that she was healthy overshadowed the fact that she was a girl. It meant there was still the opportunity to yet have more children, perhaps boys.

But when Becca arrived, the doctors told her *maem*, "No more." The fact that Becca was the last child, even if she wasn't a son, meant that her parents, especially Maem, pampered and spoiled her in ways that shocked even Kate.

Kate wiped her hands on her work apron as she finished washing the last milk bucket. She smiled at Miriam, and together they walked to the back room where the hay was neatly stacked.

"Beware Becca," Miriam whispered. "She's in a wild mood this morning."

Kate gave a soft chuckle. When wasn't Becca in a wild mood? Becca was not a morning person. Why should today be an exception? The buttons on her overcoat were not aligned properly and a long strand of hair fell from her bun. She wore nothing over her head and her cheeks bore the marks from her pillow. She barely grumbled hello as she grabbed a pitchfork and started mucking the horse and mule stalls.

"*Danke* for the warning," Kate whispered back, unable to hide the teasing tone of her voice.

As Kate and Miriam broke the bales of hay into large flakes for the horse and mules, they could hear Becca grumbling to herself. It took all of Kate's self-restraint not to giggle at her youngest sister's fiery personality and ability to make a mountain out of any molehill.

"You're giving them too much," Miriam scolded, watching as Becca carelessly tossed fresh shavings into the stall.

"Oh, hush yourself!" Becca retorted, ignoring Kate's raised eyebrow. "Maybe they're extra hungry today! Did you ever think of that?" As if to prove her point, she tossed another shovelful of pine shavings into the horse's stall.

Miriam rolled her eyes.

It was seven when the chores were almost finished and Daed excused the girls. Miriam and Becca needed to change out of their work dresses for school. Kate followed them across the yard as they hurried into the house, Becca outrunning Miriam by a long shot. Kate smiled, wondering why Becca was in such a hurry anyway. If Kate knew her sister, she'd be complaining about having to walk to school as soon as she was out the door.

Inside the house, Kate paused at the sink in the mudroom to wash her hands and kick off her work boots. No sense tracking dirt through the house, forcing Maem to get out the broom. Removing the black knit scarf she had worn for chores, she smoothed down a few stray strands of hair before putting on her head covering, taking a straight pin from the front of her dress to secure it in place.

She greeted her *maem* with a smile. "Need help?"

"*Nee*," Maem responded. The table was already set and plates of food put out. All that was needed was the family to take their places.

Without being asked, Kate removed one of the chairs near the head of the table and set it by the sofa. She didn't know why they didn't just leave it there, but Maem insisted that everything had its place and the place for that chair was at the table unless they were eating.

David's place, Kate thought as she looked around, wondering where he was.

"He's not out yet, then?"

Maem glanced over her shoulder at Kate, her despondent eyes answering for her. Then she shook her head.

"Mayhaps I'll see if he needs any help."

She rapped her knuckles on the closed bedroom door at the bottom of the staircase. Once, twice. When no one answered, she placed her hand on the doorknob and hesitated. Her chest lifted and fell as she took a deep breath before turning it and gently pushing open the door.

"David?" She peered into the room, dark from the drawn shades.

"Go away."

In the dim light, Kate could just make out his form, still laying in bed. After the accident, Maem and Daed had moved out of their bedroom on the first floor so that David would not have to navigate the stairs every day. Without her parents' double bed and faded navy quilt, the room looked strange to Kate. Stranger still was the fact that it was occupied by her younger brother now, his disability making it impossible for him to get upstairs anymore.

"Are you still in bed, then?" As always, she tried to sound cheerful as she headed to the window, her hand outstretched to touch the simple green shade.

"Do not raise that!"

She ignored him. Light flooded the room and she turned, just in time to see him dart under the covers. The borrowed wheelchair lay overturned by the far side of the bed. Had he tried to get up by himself and failed? She bent over to pick it up and set it properly on its wheels. "Now, let's get you up and dressed for the day," she said, reaching her hand out to take the edge of the quilt and peel it back.

"Why bother?" He managed to flip onto his side so that his back faced her. "To just sit in a chair all day? I might as well stay in bed."

Kate took a deep breath and reached for his arm. Thankfully, he didn't fight her as she pulled him upright and into a sitting position. "Shall we start by getting dressed?" She didn't wait for an answer and turned toward the clothes hanging from pegs on the wall: black trousers and a white button-down shirt. "Let's go," she commanded as she handed him the shirt.

He glared at her, his dark eyes flashing. "Now you want to tell me what to do?"

The way he emphasized the word *now* hurt. She knew what he meant. The implied accusation cut her to the quick. Over the past few weeks, she found herself struggling to fight the urge to avoid him and his hateful words. God wanted her to tend to David. Kate knew this from her private prayers with Him. So whenever David hurled comments full of spite and misery, she pretended she didn't hear his words and continued fussing about his room as if everything was perfectly normal.

It wasn't.

"Looks to be nice out today," she heard herself say casually, glancing out the window. "Sunny and warm enough to finish melting the snow, I think."

No response.

She turned around and noticed that he hadn't moved. "*Ja vell*," she said. "I'll give you some privacy to change and then Daed can help you into your wheelchair." She forced a smile that she didn't feel inside of her heart as she walked toward the door. "Five minutes enough?" Without waiting for an answer, she left the room, leaving the door just slightly ajar so that he knew someone would be back momentarily.

The morning ritual of dealing with David wore on Kate's nerves. The anger that flashed in his eyes mirrored the perpetual guilt that she felt. One decision about one buggy ride had altered so many lives, she often told herself while she lay awake in bed, staring at shadows dancing on the ceiling from moonlight beaming through the window. She rarely found a restful sleep as this thought haunted her, a constant reminder of what her silence had done to her family.

Still, she vowed that she would not fail David or her parents. Even if no one discussed it, she accepted responsibility for her role in the accident and promised herself that she would be there, always, to help tend to David and his needs.

Back in the kitchen, Kate inhaled the familiar smells of Maem's breakfast. The scent of freshly baked bread lingered in the air and she shut her eyes, savoring that moment. As soon as breakfast began, the day would shift into full gear, and the never-ending seasonal farm chores with Daed would begin.

Kate dreaded fertilizing the fields. Spreading manure was not the most pleasant job, by any stretch of the imagination. Still, it needed to be done, especially before planting. While Daed drove the team of Belgian mules, Kate was responsible for clearing any brush from in front of the machinery, an important task since they hadn't worked in the back field for two seasons, permitting it to have fallow time.

But now, especially with the increasing debt due to David's unexpected medical bills, they needed that field to yield some crops. Amish Aid only covered so much of David's expenses. The rest came out of pocket. Daed's pocket, anyway.

She had wanted to work in the market again this spring. The previous year, she'd had the chance to travel with the youth group that worked in Flemington, New Jersey, at the farmers' market. It was a big, bustling place with multiple stores where Amish vendors from a variety of communities came to sell crafts, cheese, baked goods, and meats. Kate's job had been to work at the market's restaurant. She'd found that, despite the funny looks and sometimes silly questions from the non-Amish patrons, she'd enjoyed her time away from the farm and with her friends.

This year, she would not be returning to Flemington. Without David's help to work alongside Daed, Kate had no choice. It wasn't even discussed, just assumed. And while nary a complaint crossed her lips, her heart felt heavy when she realized that her contribution to David's bills was not in tangible money but in providing surrogate labor for her *daed*—labor that was nowhere near as helpful as David's had once been.

"He's ready for Daed?"

Kate met her *maem*'s gaze and nodded. "*Ja*, he's getting changed."

Maem pressed her lips together but did not reply. She didn't have to say a word. Kate could read her mind. God's will was one thing. David's attitude was quite another. Still, Maem tended to keep things to herself, refusing to share her thoughts aloud. The tension in the house said enough on her behalf.

The door slammed shut behind Becca as she raced into the kitchen. Her eyes shone bright and she quickly assessed the table. "Pancakes today?"

Maem smiled. "Thought your *daed* and Kate could use the extra something special for breakfast before fertilizing that field."

Dramatically, Becca flopped into her chair and rested her head against her hand. "Shouldn't going to school earn me something special?"

Kate tried to maintain a serious look, but a smile crept across her face. "Oh, Becca," she said lightly. "Since you are having pancakes, too, seems mighty special for all of us!"

Just as Becca was forming a retort, a loud noise from the back bedroom interrupted their conversation. Kate glanced at her *maem* before hurrying toward the bedroom. This time, she did not knock as she flung the door open and peered inside for the second time that morning.

The wheelchair was on its side at the foot of the bed. David lay sprawled beside it on the floor. Incapable of moving his legs by himself, he was tangled in bedsheets that had fallen to the floor with him. He tried to lift himself up, pulling at the side of the bed for support.

"David!"

"Look what you've done now!" The fury in his eyes burned through her. "You left me alone. Once again, Kate! You left me alone!"

She turned her head, as if his words were a hand that slapped her cheek. Lowering her eyes, she took a step backward, her shoulders brushing against the door as her *maem* rushed past her and hurried to David's side.

"Now, now," she tried to soothe. "I'm sure that Kate had nothing to do with this."

He glared at her. "It's all her fault!"

Maem shook her head and gently clicked her tongue. "Just a little overzealous this morning, David. You should have waited for Daed."

"Hurry up and wait! Hurry up and wait!" He pushed at her hand as Maem tried to help him. "That's all I do anymore. What's the point?"

"What's done is done . . ." she started to say, ignoring his complaints as she righted the wheelchair. Then, with strong arms, Maem lifted David upright, placing him none too gently into the seat. Kate cringed as she watched, knowing the effort it took to move David's dead weight. With deft hands, Maem quickly straightened his shirt, rebuttoning the top two buttons that he had lined up improperly, and then place a crocheted lap blanket across his knees.

"There! All set for breakfast!"

Kate lowered her eyes and turned around, not able to swallow the hurt in her throat from David's stinging comments. She couldn't imagine where Maem found the strength to sound so cheerful all of the time. Kate tried to emulate her, finding a solid role model in her *maem*'s attitude, but it was a journey Kate knew would not be completed overnight.

Breakfast was a solemn affair. Daed sat quietly at the head of the table, lowering his head for the premeal prayer. Everyone else followed his example. Everyone except David. Kate snuck a peek at him as she feigned closing her eyes and noticed that he stared straight ahead, defiant and angry. It did not bode for a happy day in the Zook house. Suddenly, fertilizing the back field didn't seem like such an unpleasant chore after all.

CHAPTER THREE

By the time Friday rolled around, the temperatures had risen and spring seemed fully under way. The air felt warm and dry, a welcome respite from the awful cold winter they had just survived. Everyone was anxious for spring this year, Kate especially.

It was not an ordinary weekday because Becca and Miriam were home from school. There was only one teacher who taught in their one-room schoolhouse, and, on this occasion, she'd left to go visit relatives in Ohio for a few days. The girls had happily accepted an extralong weekend, even thought it meant they'd have to spend the spare time doing farmwork.

At the breakfast table, Daed gave the assignments, making it clear that he was going to take advantage of having extra hands at home to assist him with his work. It had been expected, of course. A day off from school didn't mean that Becca and Miriam would be idle. That, however, did not stop their mouths from dropping when Daed told Kate that the two younger girls, not Kate, would help with the fence repair in the fields that afternoon. Kate felt overjoyed at the announcement because it meant she'd get to work in the garden. To her, nothing was better than time spent tending the crops.

"Fixing the fence?" Becca repeated in disbelief. "Yuck!"

"Becca!" Maem scolded, a disapproving look in her eyes.

Kate tried to hide her smile. Leave it to Becca to get away with such talk. Sassy back talk was Becca's specialty, that was for sure and certain. Kate knew that her *maem* would never have accepted such lip from herself or her older *bruder*, Thomas, when they'd been that age. Time had softened her parents, apparently, and the result was Becca's tendency to say what everyone was thinking but refrained from sharing.

From the pout on Becca's face, Kate knew that her youngest sister wasn't finished. "Fixing fences is hard! And boring!" She crossed her arms over her chest and scowled. "Besides, that's man's work!"

Kate caught her breath. *Of course it was man's work*, she thought. And it took two men to do it properly, one to hold the boards or wire while the other nailed it to the posts. The problem at the Zook farm was that there was only one man to do everything. Becca's reminder hit home for everyone.

Discreetly, Kate glanced in David's direction and saw his face twist into a disgusted expression. He narrowed his eyes at Becca's proclamation and pushed himself away from the breakfast table, struggling with the wheelchair as he tried to retreat to his bedroom.

"Now look what you did," Miriam whispered harshly in Becca's direction.

"What?" She looked genuinely confused. "What did I say?"

Miriam rolled her eyes while Maem shook her head. "Becca, you need to mind your words. '*Whoever keeps his mouth and his tongue, keeps himself out of trouble.*'"

Without a word, Daed stood up and disappeared out the front door, leaving his plate half-finished and the women to deal with David. Kate watched him leave, his shoulders slouched over and a forlorn expression on his face. Her heart hurt as she shut her eyes, praying silently that God would ease Daed's pain.

After helping her *maem* clean the dishes, Kate hurried outside. She didn't want to miss one minute of time spent alone in the garden, her hoe in hand, as she picked at the soil, turning it over and pulling out any rocks and roots that rose to the surface.

Not five minutes had passed when she heard the porch door open and saw the two younger girls emerge from the house. Becca jumped down the steps in one big leap, falling to her knees. Scrambling to her feet, she made a face in Kate's direction before calling out, "Lucky!"

Kate rolled her eyes, trying to not let Becca's jealousy bother her.

While Becca ran toward the barn, Miriam took the long route, walking up the slight incline to the garden plot. She lingered by the edge, her bare feet digging into the freshly tilled soil where she stood. There was a look of longing in her eyes as she watched Kate work the soil.

"I'd help you, Kate," Miriam said, a sense of sadness in her voice. "But Daed wants us to help with the fencing."

Kate nodded, her eyes still focused on the dirt and her hands on the wooden handle of her hoe. *There was so much work to do*, she thought, that Miriam's help would have been most welcome. Still, she didn't mind doing it alone. "*Danke*, Miriam."

She knew that either of her younger sisters would have switched places with her in a heartbeat. Repairing fences was hard work that brought little gratification. There was no breeze, and the sun would be hot on top of the hill by the upper field where the cows grazed. Daed tended to focus on work, so there would be no singing of hymns or idle chatter as they worked. His serious nature did not lend itself to jovial pastimes, especially since the accident.

In the garden, however, Kate could breathe freer without the stern eyes of her father upon her. There was ample shade from the nearby oak tree. Birds played in the branches, chirping in spring delight as they readied their nests for babies. The more remote location meant that she wouldn't have to listen to cars racing down the road or stop to chat with visiting neighbors. It also meant that she didn't have to see the place where the broken and battered buggy remained. From the top of the grazing paddock, where they'd be tending the fence, a view of it was unavoidable.

No one spoke much about that night or how it had affected their lives. But surely her family knew that it bothered her to see the wreckage, a constant reminder of what had happened on that snowy night in December. It dawned on Kate that, mayhaps, Daed excused her from the fencing repair chore to save her from having to see the damaged buggy. Initially, she thought he'd asked her to work on the garden because he knew how much she loved doing it. Now, she wasn't so sure.

Leaning against the hoe, she stared down at the freshly tilled soil. Her mind worked rapidly as she tried to determine whether that was important. Was Daed actually trying to protect her from the memory or merely avoiding her presence? Probably the former, she decided. As Maem always said, "What's done is done. Best to move on."

"Kate Zook!"

Startled from her thoughts, she looked up, surprised to see her friend, Verna Lapp, walking around the barn and toward her. With her dark-blue dress and black apron, Verna looked older than Kate remembered. After all, they had grown up together, attending school as young girls and their first singing as young adults. Their friendship seemed grounded in their ability to balance their differences. Verna's blond hair and blue eyes contrasted against Kate's dark ones. Verna was outgoing and adventuresome while Kate preferred staying close to home. Yet their friendship had persevered throughout the years.

Indeed, Verna had always been Kate's special friend, a sister on a different level than Miriam or Becca could ever achieve. However, as Kate watched Verna approach, she realized that she hadn't seen much of her friend since December. *By whose choice*, she wondered, and then realized that it had most likely been her own.

"*Wie geht's?*" Verna reached out her hand to shake Kate's, a common greeting among friends.

Kate tried to smile, fighting her own sense of culpability in having ignored her friendship. Where had the time gone? How many months had gone by without any visits to her friends' homes or excursions to youth gatherings? The guilt caused her to look down at her feet, ashamed that she had neglected others in such a manner.

"Getting the garden ready for planting," she said, gesturing to her hoe. As soon as she said it, she felt foolish, realizing that was not the answer to the question Verna asked.

"I can see that, silly," Verna laughed, her eyes bright and freckles already covering her nose. "I meant in general. How are you doing?"

Kate shrugged, unable to verbalize a response to the question. How could she share with Verna the burden of guilt that weighed on her shoulders? It seemed impossible to explain. So she remained silent.

"Haven't seen you in a while. Just saw your *daed* up yonder," she said, glancing over her shoulder in the direction of the top field. "Said you were down here, so thought I'd pop in to see you."

"Right kind of you," Kate managed to say.

An awkward silence fell between them. Kate wasn't certain whether she was happy about Verna's surprise visit. It was easier to not see her friends, she realized . . . part of her wasn't ready to admit that life continued on, even though Maem continually reminded her of this. No matter what happened, God's plans continued to work for the betterment of His creation. Hiding at home would not stop that, she scolded herself. "Been a long winter, *ja*?" Verna didn't wait for an answer. "Mayhaps time to get you back into the fold for singings."

Kate shook her head. "I . . . I'm just not ready yet."

"Oh fiddle-faddle!" Verna dismissed Kate's confession with a wave of her hand. "There's nothing to be ready about, Kate. I told your *daed* that there's a singing at the Yoders' after worship on Sunday. Sure would be nice if you came." She leaned forward and lowered her voice. "You are missed."

"I can't face everyone," she managed to reply.

"Whatever for?" Verna laughed. "Everyone asks about you."

Everyone? The thought of people wondering about her, asking how she fared, struck Kate as odd. Surely they all had heard the story by now. Surely they all knew that she, Kate Zook, had not stopped David from killing Ruth. That she, and she alone, could have prevented the accident. Oh, she lived each day remembering that she had wisely removed herself from the seat of danger, while knowingly permitting another to go in her place.

"I'm sure," was all she managed to say.

"Well, your *daed* said he'd talk to you about it."

Oh, Kate could only imagine that he would. She didn't reply.

"Sadie Esh took your place at market," Verna said, changing the conversation. "Her other *schwester* is working there, too. At the bakery, I heard."

Samuel's sisters? Kate tried to ignore the stab of regret she felt to hear her place had been taken. She missed her days working at the market's restaurant and felt a momentary wave of resentment that she had been so easily replaced. Immediately, she shoved that thought aside. After all, she shouldn't have been surprised. With Kate unable to work, the restaurant had to fill a spot. Amish markets like the one in Flemington were increasingly popular with the Englische, many of whom drove long distances to purchase Amish goods. It was only natural that Kate's absence created a void that needed to be filled.

"Elmer asked me first, but I just didn't feel right taking your job. Sure would have been fun if both of us could have gone."

"*Ja*," Kate responded, a longing tone in her voice. The early morning drives to market had meant she didn't need to help with chores. At night, when she had returned, she always had such fun stories to share with Miriam and Becca. Maem, of course, never wanted to hear anything about the Englische and markets. She'd turned her back on them twelve years ago after Jacob died. No one ever challenged her on that, especially Kate.

"Oh *vell*," Verna said, waving her hand dismissively. Leave it to Verna to always see the bright side of things. "I have enough to do at home, what with helping my *maem* and working on my tie quilts for donating to the Mennonite Central Committee. And to sell, of course."

"That's nice," Kate said, a wistful look in her eyes.

Last year, they made over fifty quilts for the MCC, which sold them in order to fund their efforts helping communities in need. Using a foot-operated sewing machine, Verna and Kate pieced quilt tops made from old clothing that people donated to the cause. Dresses, shirts, aprons, and pants were cut into four-by-four squares and sewed together, making simple patterns. Unlike many of the quilts that the tourists sought and bought, the simple nature of these tie quilts lent themselves to more functionality in the Amish home. Besides being easier to make, they were plain and warm, with thick fleece backing and plump batting inside.

"You should come over to help. I'm tying a bunch of quilts on Monday and Tuesday. We could spend the afternoon on it." Verna smiled before she added, "Like old times."

"I'd love to help, Verna," Kate admitted, meaning it on more than one level. "But Daed needs my help here. We just fertilized the back field last week. I reckon we'll begin tilling the soil before planting corn week next."

Disappointment crossed Verna's face, a sincere look that spoke volumes about her affection for Kate. "Ah *vell*," she said, lowering her eyes. "If anything changes, you just come on over, *ja*? And I'll be working on the quilts on Mondays throughout the spring and summer. The invitation remains open, Kate. You know that."

"I know that, Verna." Oh, how she would have loved to be able to help Verna with the quilts. Just like the old days—the days before the accident when life held some semblance of normalcy.

In hindsight, Kate wasn't certain that life had ever really been normal on the farm. Too much was left unspoken. It had been for years. The only one who seemed to enjoy being honest about the family's difficulties was David, but, despite his apparent delight in constantly rehashing painful memories, even he knew what line not to cross in the sand.

Of course, all of that was a moot point now. Their family situation would never even approach normal again, not now. So there was no sense in acting like she could consider accepting Verna's invitation. Kate knew that Daed would need her help with chores, even if it rained. Running a farm required a lot of work and many hands to complete it. Even when David had been strong and capable, Kate would have been asked to labor alongside them. Now that it was just her and Daed, Kate had no idea what to expect besides endless days of hard work and nights of restless sleep. While she dreaded the former, she eagerly anticipated the latter.

"Good to see you, Verna," she said, her voice barely audible. "You be sure to send my best to your family, *ja*?"

Verna nodded. "And don't forget about the Sunday singing, Kate. Might do you some good to get back to socializing a bit, *ja*?" Verna did not wait for a response. Instead, she waved her hand and began walking down the driveway toward the road.

With a forlorn feeling in her heart, Kate watched as Verna disappeared. She hadn't realized how much she missed her friends until just now. For months, her focus on the family had outweighed anything else. Time for socializing simply ceased to exist.

During those initial days after the accident, David's recovery took all of Maem's energy and Kate had felt compelled to step in, helping with both the housework and the barn chores while her *maem* stayed at the hospital with her son. When David finally returned home, Maem managed to keep up with the housework so that Kate could spend more time in the barn helping Daed. However, Kate saw the toll that it took on Miriam as well as Maem, so she had done her best to do as much as she could to eliminate stress by taking on more work.

It was exhausting.

Only, she hadn't realized how exhausting it truly was until this very moment. By sacrificing everything in order to help at home, she had lost out on much more than she'd realized. As she picked up the hoe and returned her attention to the garden, she reminded herself that she was not the only one making a sacrifice. Everyone in the family had made concessions in their lives to accommodate David's disability. *Of course*, she thought as she uprooted a large stick, *Ruth had made the ultimate sacrifice.*

Chapter Four

"After you finish at Susan's, I need you to go to the Esh farm," Maem told her before Kate headed out the door.

Kate stopped and stared at her mother in surprise. "Whatever for?" She hoped her question didn't sound sassy. It wasn't like her to question her *maem*. Despite the Esh farm only being two farms away from Susan's, walking there and back would take at least forty-five minutes. "It's awful far, Maem."

"Take the scooter with the basket, then." Maem's arms were covered in flour as she kneaded the bread for the next two days' meals. With tomorrow being Sunday, there would be no baking permitted. "She has my Tupperware and I need it for service tomorrow. Promised to bring cupcakes for the *kinner*."

Inwardly, Kate groaned. All that way for Tupperware? And using the kick scooter? It wasn't as if Maem didn't have other containers to carry baked goods to worship service.

"And she'll send you home with roots for the garden. I want to get those planted this afternoon when you return."

Ah, Kate thought. *The real reason.*

Maem had a knack for gardening, especially when it came to perennials. Neighbors often thought of her when their perennial vegetables sprouted too much and they divided them to share with others. Kate wasn't sure why, but when it came to extras, Maem was always first in line. She could walk through her perennial garden, the one that was closer to the house than the larger one under the oak tree, and point out who had donated what to her collection. Her pride showed when she shared the tales of the people who gave her starter roots for asparagus, rhubarb, kale, and leeks. And she always pointed out her cherished black-eyed Susans and wild mint tea plants.

There would be no talking Maem out of the journey now, Kate reasoned.

Upon arriving at Susan's, Kate immediately felt a weight lift from her shoulders. The airy house, so different than Maem and Daed's older farmhouse, welcomed her. The back wall of the kitchen held large windows, letting in the light so that it flooded the white linoleum floor with rays of bright sun. Since the house was more contemporary, the rooms were bigger and the ceilings a touch higher. The ambiance warmed her heart and made her feel refreshed.

"Susan?" she called out, her eyes immediately falling on the plates in the sink. Without waiting for direction, she began to tackle that task. Best to get started, she told herself.

A few minutes later, she heard her *aendi*'s footsteps on the stairs. Ruth Ann gurgled in Susan's arms, while Kate quickly dried her hands on a towel and reached out for the baby.

"Sorry 'bout the dishes," Susan mumbled. "Tough night last one."

"*Ja?*"

Susan nodded. "The *boppli* kept me up. Teething, I think."

Kate nuzzled at the baby's neck, smiling when Ruth Ann cooed in her ear. "She's such an angel," Kate replied. "I can't imagine she could be anything less."

"If you don't mind watching her, I'll head out to help Timothy. He's out readying the fields for planting."

"Bit early for planting, *ja*?"

Susan shrugged. Timothy wasn't originally from Lancaster County. His family had been living in Indiana when he was born. When his grandfather died, the family farm was left to one of his older brothers. Luckily, an uncle of Timothy's, who only had daughters, asked him to move to Pennsylvania to help on his farm.

In a day and age of not enough farmland, Timothy had happily accepted the offer. When his uncle had passed away, he'd been more than willing to purchase it. However, the word on the Amish grapevine was that the purchase price was higher than Timothy expected. As a result, he held a big bank note, which meant long days in the fields praying for good crops to pay it off. No one liked having debt, especially Timothy and Susan.

It often made Kate wonder what Daed would do with the farm as he got older. With her elder *bruder*, Thomas, already settled on his own farm and David clearly unable to take on the responsibility to manage the property, Daed would have to sell it eventually.

If the farm was sold, they would lose their life right to stay there until they died. And who knew what would become of them then? They'd be dependent on their son-in-laws, whoever they turned out to be—with Becca and Miriam still so young, and Kate still unattached, it was anyone's guess what sort of husbands they'd secure. And the son-in-laws would not just have to care for them as they aged, but also for David, whose disability was never going to disappear. It was a burden that neither Maem nor Daed wanted to face.

Of course, the prospect of selling the farm was many years in the future. Becca would need to be settled down before such a thing happened. And there was always the chance that one of the girls might marry an aspiring farmer without a farm, although such situations were few and far between these days. Young men and boys were groomed to take over their family farm; the rest learned a trade. Unmarried, farmless farmers were not an easy-to-find commodity in their area. And the right young man would need to do more than just take on their farm—he'd have to be willing to take on two aging parents and a disabled brother as well.

For the rest of the morning, Kate split her time between tending to Ruth Ann's needs and cleaning the kitchen. She made certain to scrub the floor, getting even the corners, which seemed to have gathered extra dust bunnies since she had last visited. Then, she hurried upstairs to grab the dirty clothing from the baby's room. She washed the tiny items by hand and set them to dry in the sun. By the time the afternoon sun began to dip in the sky, Kate had the downstairs of the house in order, Ruth Ann's clean clothes were hanging from small hangers on pegs in her room, and a warm meal was waiting in the oven for Susan and Timothy.

The look of appreciation on Susan's tired and dirty face said it all. "Back field is ready for seeding," she announced when she walked into the kitchen, heading directly to the sink to wash her hands and face. She took the proffered towel from Kate and rubbed it against the back of her neck. "One of the mules broke the harness, though. Timothy went to Yonie's shop to see if he might fix it yet."

Kate exhaled, knowing that, if they couldn't get it fixed, they would not be able to plant the field on Monday. *Always something*, she thought as she put on her shoes, getting ready for the long scooter ride to the Esh farm.

She took the back roads, thankful that she wouldn't have to pass the broken buggy on the way. For that, she was grateful. For some reason, passing it on the way down the hill didn't bother her half as much as it did on her return trip. There was something about walking that same road in the same direction that caused Kate enormous grief. Avoiding it today meant a lot to her.

"Why, Kate Zook!" Mary smiled as she opened the screen door, the hinges creaking just a little. "Your *maem* mentioned you'd be stopping by. That's an awful long walk from your house!" She peered over Kate's shoulder and clicked her tongue. "Mayhaps my Samuel can take you back, then!"

Kate felt her heart flutter at the mention of Samuel. She wasn't certain why. "*Nee, nee,*" she tried to reassure his *maem*. "I have my scooter. Didn't take much time at all." The last thing she wanted was for Samuel Esh to be bothered into harnessing his horse to take her home.

"Oh nonsense!" Mary took ahold of her arm and pulled her inside the house. "*Kum esse!* I have some freshly baked cookies. You can taste test them before the *kinner* devour them!"

Within seconds, Kate found herself seated on the family bench at the kitchen table, a plate of warm, gooey chocolate chip cookies in front of her, and Mary Esh chattering away as if they were long-lost friends. A large woman with a round belly, Mary was known throughout the *g'may* for her effervescent personality. Always happy and laughing, Mary looked at the bright side in every situation.

"I heard your *daed* started his spring planting already!"

Kate shook her head. "*Nee,* not yet. Another week, I reckon."

She clicked her tongue. Tsk-tsk. "Not even the middle of April! Why, he's getting a jump start on all of us!" She laughed. "He'll be sitting under an oak tree drinking meadow tea while the rest of us are playing catch-up!"

Kate smiled as a way of response. She had never seen her *daed* sitting under any tree drinking anything! The visual almost made her laugh.

"How's your *maem* doing, anyway? Haven't seen her much since . . ." Mary let her voice trail off, the words unspoken.

"Maem's strong," Kate heard herself say. "She's doing well."

"Oh help!" Mary hurried to the oven and pulled down the door. The delicious smell of more cookies floated throughout the room. "I almost burnt them! My word!" The diversion helped to change the subject as Mary quickly reached inside, using a triple-folded towel as a pot holder to remove the metal sheet covered with cookies. "Just in time!"

"I shouldn't be distracting you," Kate said, starting to rise from the bench.

"Nonsense, Kate! I'm just getting addle brained as I age." She set the cookie sheet on the wooden counter. "Happens to the best of us, I reckon."

The hinge of the screen door squeaked, announcing the arrival of someone else. Kate lowered her eyes, wondering who it was and dreading having to socialize more than she already had. Mary Esh had eleven *kinner*, Samuel falling somewhere in the middle, so that meant there were plenty of children still living at home. She hoped it was one of the younger ones.

"Who's here, Maem?"

As luck had it, Joshua peeked around the corner. Roughly the same age as Becca, Joshua was a good foot taller than her younger sister but had the same gleam in his eye. Kate gathered from the stories she heard about his antics at the school yard that he shared her fiery temperament.

"Why, Kate Zook!" He answered his own question as he sauntered into the kitchen, his fingers hooked around his suspenders and a grin on his face. "Ain't seen you about since the accident!" He ignored the stern look Mary tossed in his direction. "What brings you a-calling?"

"Never you mind," Mary said, trying to chase him away. "Go run down the basement stairs and fetch me that Tupperware with her *maem*'s name on it." He gave his *maem* a pleading look, obviously wanting to linger longer to talk with Kate. "Go on now! Get!"

Disappointed, he scampered across the floor, like a puppy with his tail between his legs, and disappeared down the wooden stairs.

"That boy!" Mary shook her head, tsking her tongue three times. "He's so much like his older *bruder*! Worries me, that! Gonna travel and give me a plain ole heart attack, I know it!"

Kate knew better than to ask which brother she referenced. Certainly, Mary meant Samuel. While he had other brothers, none of them had decided to explore the world of the Englische.

Sighing, Mary turned back to Kate. "Sure am sorry that the girls aren't here to visit. Sadie and Katie are at market in Maryland, although they are a bit younger than you, *ja*?" She didn't wait for an answer. "And the other boys are out in the field, I'm sure. Although they wouldn't have much of interest to say." She laughed at her own comment. "Fields, crops, barns, and buggies. That's about the extent of it!"

The loud thumping of bare feet on the wooden steps announced Joshua's return. He grinned at Kate as he handed the Tupperware to his *maem* and slid into a seat across from their visitor. Without moving his eyes, he reached out, snatched a cookie, and popped it into his mouth.

"You staying for supper, then?"

"Joshua! Go find your *bruder*! Need him to harness the buggy to take Kate home." Mary placed her hands on his shoulders and redirected him out of his seat. "And I see those cookie crumbs on your lips. That's one less for you after dinner, you little rascal!"

"Aw, Maem!"

Kate suppressed a smile as Mary shooed him out the door.

"That boy!" Mary shook her head. "Maybe a little exposure to the world might do him some good after all." She glanced out the window. "Did a whole lot of good for Samuel, that's for sure and certain."

If Kate wanted to ask what Mary meant by that, she didn't. Prying was not something she was prone to do. But Mary's comment piqued her curiosity. In his younger years, Samuel might have been bitten by the wanderlust bug, but he had sure hightailed it home and walked the straight and narrow ever since. She certainly couldn't recall him acting anything like his outspoken younger brother, Joshua.

"I best get going, then," Kate said, breaking the silence. "Maem will need help with supper."

"You just stay right there a spell." Mary leaned out the window and called for Samuel to hurry up. "He's harnessing the mare to take you home. It'll be faster."

Hating to feel like a burden, Kate ran her fingers nervously along the waist of her apron as if smoothing out wrinkles, although none were there. If only Samuel had been out in the fields. If only Maem had sent Miriam. If only . . .

A little voice inside of her head reprimanded her: *Don't live on what-ifs!*

Five minutes later, Kate sensed someone watching her. The back of her neck felt warm and she turned around, startled to see Samuel standing in the doorway, leaning against the frame with his hands in his pockets. His eyes, such a deep, dark blue, looked directly into hers. The expression on his face was thoughtful.

"Someone in need of a ride home, then?"

She felt color flood to her cheeks. "I have my scooter. I don't need a ride, but . . ." She couldn't finish the sentence and lowered her eyes.

"Nonsense, Kate!" Mary turned to face her son. "Just as easy for you to take her home, ain't so? 'Sides, you can swing by the Millers' farm for me, can't you now? Pick up some eggs. We're almost out and won't make it to Monday."

He nodded his head, his gaze still on Kate. "Will do, Maem." He paused, just for a moment, before a slight smile crossed his lips. "Ready then, Kate?" Without waiting for a response, he shifted his body toward the door and took a step away from the kitchen. "Let's go."

Quietly, she stood up and made her way to the door, stopping only to pick up the Tupperware and to thank Mary Esh for the cookies. Then, with downcast eyes, Kate hurried after Samuel who walked across the yard slowly, as if waiting for her to catch up to him.

In silence, they walked side by side to the buggy, Kate keeping her distance from him and wishing that she could have just ridden home on her scooter. Leaning against the wall, it looked inviting. However, Mary also needed eggs, so the trip was not a complete waste of Samuel's time.

As if reading her mind, Samuel gestured toward the buggy, indicating that she should get in as he set the small box of roots on the backseat. "I'll fetch your scooter, Kate." Obediently, she did as he instructed and climbed into the buggy, setting the Tupperware on the seat beside her.

"There now," he said when he set the scooter in the back of the buggy, leaving the plastic window rolled up so that a fresh breeze could keep them cool. He took a deep breath, walked around to the driver's side, and in a quick motion, jumped inside and sat beside her. She noticed that he moved the Tupperware onto the floor, pushing it just enough under the seat so that they wouldn't kick it.

"You mind if I stop at Millers' farm first, Kate?"

She glanced at him, surprised to see him waiting in anticipation of her answer. Shaking her head, she looked away. "That's fine, I reckon." She wasn't certain why he wanted to do that. The Miller farm was just past her *daed*'s farm. It would have been easier to drop her off first, but she wasn't about to say that.

For the first few minutes, they rode in silence. Hair from the rump of the horse floated through the opened front window and Kate wiped at her mouth.

"You getting a mouthful?"

She laughed. "*Ja*, I sure am."

He reached up and shut the window. "Better?"

She nodded.

"Funny, ain't it?" He chuckled to himself. "Have barely seen you at all in months and only at worship. Now it's been twice in one week."

She thought that, technically, it had been more than a week since he'd given her that ride home in his buggy, but she didn't correct him.

"Must be a sign!" he teased and nudged her gently with his elbow.

She blushed and looked out the window.

"Aw, I'm just kidding, Kate. Trying to get a smile out of you. Takes more muscles to frown than to smile. Did you know that?" He returned his attention to driving the horse. Another horse and buggy approached them and Samuel lifted his hand, waving a silent hello as a greeting. "Sure is nice out. What a difference a week makes, *ja*?"

She nodded, not trusting herself to speak. He made her feel nervous, his constant questions and gentle teasing.

"There's a singing tomorrow after church."

It wasn't a question, just a simple statement. However, his silence compelled her to respond. "Verna stopped by and told me."

"You going, then?"

Kate shrugged. "Doubt it. Need to help Daed in the fields on Monday." Most likely, they'd be up by four thirty in the morning to tackle the milking and start the field work before breakfast. Miriam and Becca would clean the stalls when they awoke. It would be a long few days, that was for sure and certain.

"I reckon you won't be the only one doing field work on Monday morning." He pursued the topic no further.

They rode the rest of the way to the Millers' farm in silence. Kate wondered whether he was sorry that he hadn't dropped her off first. She wished she felt comfortable enough to engage in a conversation with him. She wanted to thank him again for the ride home the previous week, to thank him for sparing her from seeing the battered buggy at the accident scene once again. Yet he was too much of a stranger for her to initiate such personal conversation. The last thing she wanted was for Samuel Esh or anyone else to think she was too forward.

The Millers' farm was quiet, and for a brief moment Kate worried that no one was home. She knew she would feel terrible if Samuel had made the entire journey for naught. She glanced at him, wondering if he suspected the same thing. To her surprise, he looked unfazed. He parked the buggy and flashed her a reassuring smile.

"Be right back," he said.

She watched as he walked up the path to the barn and disappeared through a door. After several seconds, he emerged, carrying two large cartons of eggs. Carefully, he set them on the floor of the buggy, pieces of an old horse blanket wrapped protectively around the cartons so that no harm would come to the eggs on the ride back to his farm.

"They were home, then?"

He shrugged. "Don't know. I just left the money on the counter and took what we needed."

Ah, she thought. *The tried-and-true Amish honor system.* A staple of the Amish way of life. Sometimes during the hot summer months, neighbors with too many fresh tomatoes and zucchinis from their garden left extras in cartons at the end of their driveways. They'd leave a tin can nearby to collect the proceeds. If people wanted to buy any goods, they simply left money in the can and took what they wanted. Maem always clucked her tongue about that, commenting how the Englische tourists did not always play by those rules of honor. She said that if they had anything to sell, they'd sell it outright at market and only at a tended stand.

To Kate's knowledge, however, no one, not even Englische tourists, had ever stolen goods from a produce box left on the honor system.

It didn't matter, though. Maem wasn't about to encourage the tourists to stop at their farm. She was much more content to donate her excess goods to the elderly Amish who lived alone or could not farm anymore. Kate suspected that Maem's disapproval of catering to the tourists in general lay at the heart of the matter, not the supposed stealing of goods.

Anything that had to do with the Englische was taboo in the Zook household. Having been raised in a very conservative and traditional Amish home, Maem had never felt comfortable spending time among the Englische. But her desire to completely isolate herself and her family was solidified twelve years ago after the accident by the road stand. Kate didn't feel the same way about the Englische as her mother, but she understood that Maem had her reasons.

By the time he stopped the buggy in front of her house, Kate felt anxious to get out. She knew her *maem* would be wondering what had taken her so long. Surely Daed would also be needing some help with the final chores of the evening. It didn't help any when she noticed David, sitting on the porch in his wheelchair, his head pressed against his hand as he glared at Kate with his dark eyes.

Certainly her *maem* had put him there to get some fresh air. At least, Kate thought, that's what Maem would have told him.

"*Danke* for the ride," she mumbled as she started to get out of the buggy. His hand on her arm stopped her and she looked up, surprised.

"Mayhaps you'll change your mind about the singing, *ja*?"

She looked away. How could she go to the singing? How could she face the unspoken questions? How could she endure it, knowing what people were likely thinking of when they looked at her? "Mayhaps," she whispered and reached under the seat for her *maem*'s Tupperware container. Against her better instinct, she glanced at him one last time. His eyes met hers. "Mayhaps, Samuel," she repeated before turning away and hurrying into the house. She barely passed David when she heard the sound of Samuel's horse and buggy disappearing down the lane toward the road.

Avoiding David's scowl, Kate opened the door to the house and slipped inside, knowing that her brother would certainly have something to say about the fact that, while he sat on the porch, stuck in a wheelchair staring at the barren fields that he'd much prefer to be planting, she had been "joy riding" in a buggy with Samuel Esh. He'd never consider the fact that there was a good reason for it. He'd just accuse her of doing the one thing he knew he could never do again: enjoy life.

The familiar guilt burdened her as she hurried into the kitchen to see what she could do to help her *maem*.

CHAPTER FIVE

"I want you to go to the youth singing tonight."

Kate's spoon stopped in midair, her mouth open and her eyes wide. She looked at her *maem* as if questioning whether she had heard Daed properly. He hadn't asked. He hadn't suggested. He had told her. He was flat out informing her that she was to go.

Earlier that day, the family had attended worship service at the Masts' house, all of the Zooks minus David and Maem. The Masts had held the service inside their home; like most of the older farmhouses in the *g'may*, it was built specifically to accommodate large gatherings. In some of the newer homes, there were often just large rooms built over the horse barn or craft shops. But however the space worked out, the location where the worship service was held rotated. Every two weeks, worship was held in a different house within their church district.

The Masts' downstairs gathering room, emptied of its furniture and with the partitions between the kitchen and the sitting area displaced, easily accommodated the two hundred members of the *g'may* expected to participate in worship that week. Kate took her seat on the hard wooden bench. She glanced at her friend Katie Ellen who sat to her left and then turned her eyes to the center of the room where the bishop stood, his white beard moving slightly as he spoke. The sermon focused on personal forgiveness, a topic that weighed heavily in Kate's heart. She fought the urge to squirm while the bishop preached, his singsong voice rising and falling as if he were chanting and not addressing the congregation. It was a long sermon with a lot of focus on Joseph's ability to forgive his brothers after they had sold him into a life of slavery.

Kate listened intently, the color rushing to her cheeks. Had not David been sold into a similar life? A life of sitting in a wheelchair rather than courting his girl and visiting his friends? Part of her wished that David attended church with the rest of the family. Perhaps the bishop's words would have made an impression on him and helped him realize that it was time to forgive her.

When the time for silent prayer came, Kate knelt with her face pressed into her hands as she leaned against the bench. She prayed for God to provide her with the strength to remain strong for her parents and for David. She prayed for God to bless her with the wisdom and ability to handle David's temper and harsh words. And she prayed for God to grant her the insight to learn how to forgive herself the way that Joseph forgave his brothers.

After the worship service, Kate helped the hosting family with serving the food during the first sitting. No one needed to direct her in what to do. Most of the other young women knew exactly what chores to tend as well. It was their responsibility, after all, to replenish plates of fresh bread and bowls of apple butter. Kate took it upon herself to fill water cups and set them by the plates as people began to take their seats at the tables that the men had just transitioned from the worship benches. It was an easy task and one that required little, if any, interaction with her peers.

By the time the after-prayer was said over the first seating, Kate felt both hungry and tired. As a young unmarried woman, she wouldn't get to eat until the second seating in another thirty minutes. While she waited, she stood nearby, watching to see if anyone at the tables needed more water. She noticed that nobody came up to inquire if she would join them that evening at the youth singing, with the exception of Verna.

For four months, the answer from Kate remained the same: *nee*. She held no interest in attending anything social. Not now. Not yet. However, she realized that her self-isolation was taking its toll. Verna had made certain to sit beside Kate during the worship service and reiterated her invitation to both the singing and the quilting. But she'd left immediately after the worship service with her family to visit with her older brother in a neighboring district that afternoon.

Verna's absence during the fellowship time made Kate think. Clearly, the other women respected Kate's decision to distance herself, at least while she healed. However, she quickly realized that they also continued living their lives, which included friendships and social activities, things that clearly no longer involved Kate Zook.

The realization startled her, especially when she found herself relieved that her *daed* did not want to linger after the fellowship meal. Maem hadn't even come. Her parents, too, were isolating themselves.

Back at home, Kate found a chance to nap on the sofa in the main room, a sunbeam shining through the windows and warming the nape of her neck. To her surprise, when she awoke, Maem had already set the table for the evening supper and the younger *kinner* were outside, chasing the chickens into the coop with exaggerated gestures and assertive shouts.

"Why didn't you wake me, then?" she had asked her *maem* as she stretched her arms and yawned. She could hear Becca and Miriam laughing through the open window. "I would have gladly helped."

Maem smiled in return. "I know, Kate. But you looked so peaceful. I didn't have the heart . . ."

Peaceful.

A word that conjured up a whirlwind of images for Kate: Ruth Ann sleeping in her handmade pine crib, newborn kittens nursing from the mother cat's swollen belly, cows wandering in the green paddocks in springtime. Peaceful was not a twenty-year-old sleeping on the sofa while the rest of the family worked, tiptoeing around so that no one woke her. Swallowing, Kate had pushed those images from her mind. She straightened her hair as she rose from the sofa, then hurried over to help with the rest of the preparations for the meal, secretly grateful for the unexpected nap.

So, during the supper meal, when her *daed* blurted out that he wanted her to attend the youth singing that evening, Kate felt completely blindsided.

No one had mentioned youth singings in months. No one had even hinted that Kate should attend, as if there was an unspoken agreement among the family members that it was not a topic to be broached. Yet, Daed had spoken, and his words lingered in the air as if someone had painted them on canvas for all to see.

When she realized that everyone was staring at her, Kate lowered her gaze to the food on her plate. Suddenly, her appetite was no more. She set down her spoon and placed her hands on her lap. "May I be excused?"

Daed shook his head. "*Nee*, Kate. Not until you answer me."

"You didn't ask a question of me." She regretted the words the moment they slipped through her lips. *Sassy*, she scolded herself. But she did not apologize. To her surprise, he did not reprimand her. The heaviness of the tension in the room seemed to excuse the tone of her comment.

"About the singing."

She glanced at David who seemed to slouch more deeply in his wheelchair, a scowl on his face. At seventeen, he made his intention known to the family that he would never attend another singing. He would never meet up with friends and he certainly would not marry. *It's all your fault.* His words echoed in her head and her pulse quickened. How could she go to a singing, be social and laugh, enjoy life as if nothing had happened? The fact that David kept his eyes downcast did not lessen her feelings of guilt.

"I'm . . . I'm just not ready yet, Daed," she finally responded.

What she wanted to say remained in her heart, not on her lips. How could she enjoy herself at a youth singing, knowing that David remained at home? Besides, if she went to a singing, people would ask. After all, David's situation warranted an explanation and that would mean telling the story about Ruth. And what woman would want a disabled man who had caused his own injury and killed his intended bride?

"Kate," Daed said, with a firmness in his voice that indicated he meant business. "It's time."

An eerie silence fell upon the room. No forks scraping the plates. No glasses being set down. No belches of full bellies. Just silence.

Kate looked up, her eyebrows raised in surprise. Time? Time for what? She wanted to ask him the question, but words seemed trapped in her throat.

Daed must have noticed her apprehension for he took a deep breath and added, "Don't you reckon, *dochder*?"

She could feel the heat of everyone's stare upon her. Still, she could do no more than look down at her plate. She just couldn't go through with it. Not yet. While Daed might think it was time, she knew better. Part of her even suspected that that time might actually never come. Not after what she had been through.

"I can't, Daed. I just can't."

"*Ja vell,* you are going." This time, his tone took on an unusual level of severity, one that she hadn't heard in a while and certainly not one that was often directed at her. He dipped his head, poking at the food on his plate with his fork. "And that's the end of *that* discussion."

Kate felt the tears welling up in her eyes and said a quick, silent prayer that he would change his mind. As the head of the household, Daed would never accept disobedience. Not under his roof. Once he issued a command, he would accept no argument.

For the rest of suppertime, she refused to eat, merely pushing her food around the plate, and barely spoke at all, except when asked a direct question, which, thankfully, was limited to just one: "What time will you be ready?"

It was a question for which she knew there was no answer.

When the clock read four o'clock, Kate reluctantly went upstairs to change her soiled apron and fix her hair. The small mirror nailed on the wall by the door reflected her image. The dark circles under her eyes spoke of her sleepless nights while the scattering of freckles over her cheeks told stories of days spent working outside under the warm sun and blue skies. While she had never considered whether others thought she was pretty, she knew that she wasn't unattractive or overly plain. Of course, she certainly didn't think she was as striking as Esther or Verna, never mind the fact that, as of late, she knew she looked tired.

"Hi there."

Kate glanced over her shoulder, surprised to see Becca crouched on the floor by her dresser. "What are you doing there?"

She shrugged. "Didn't feel like helping with evening chores," she mumbled. Fiery little Becca looked as if she carried the weight of the world on her shoulders.

Kate stifled a laugh. "So you hid in here? Who's to say I won't tattle on you?"

Another shrug. "You won't."

She was right. Kate would offer to do the chores herself rather than rat out Becca. Moving over to the edge of her bed, Kate motioned for Becca to sit beside her. "What's up, buttercup?"

"Why do they want you to go to this stupid singing anyway?"

Kate frowned. Why would that matter to Becca? It wasn't as though Kate had never gone to a singing or social gathering before tonight. In fact, both she and David used to go out on Friday, Saturday, and Sunday evenings to visit with friends if a formal gathering had not been arranged. "Singings aren't stupid, Becca," she finally responded.

Becca snorted her thoughts about that.

"What's really bothering you?"

"Nothing's the same." Her voice sounded even younger than her ten years. The usually tough facade that Becca wore broke down as she lifted her dark eyes to stare into Kate's. "Maem's so quiet, David's always grouchy, Daed just works and sleeps. I miss the before days."

Before days and after days. That was how the Zook family segmented their lives: the days from before the accident and the days after the accident. There was no other way to split it. Before the accident, life had been different with evenings spent playing games of Scrabble or Trouble, the family gathered together and sharing a bowl of Maem's amazing popcorn, made with special seasonings and brewer's yeast.

After the accident, everything changed.

Again.

Kate understood exactly what Becca meant. The change in their home environment affected everyone, not just David. The burden on each person's back felt heavy, causing shoulders to slump forward and feet to shuffle across the floor. It was not healthy, and anything but happy. Still, it tugged at Kate's heart that Becca's world, too, had been turned upside down.

"The before days were good," Kate admitted, wrapping her arm around Becca's shoulders. "The after days will get better soon."

"When?"

"In time." It was the only answer that Kate could offer. She gently squeezed Becca, the closest gesture to a hug that she felt comfortable offering her sister. "Trust me, Becca. It will get better in time."

Becca frowned and tilted her head, looking up at her sister. "Did it ever get better after Jacob, then?"

Kate froze. *That* was unexpected. "I . . . I best finish getting ready, then," she managed to say as she stood up and returned to the small mirror. Without another word to Becca, she began fixing her hair, smoothing back any strands that escaped her tight bun.

She was only vaguely aware of Becca sighing before she shuffled out of the room, to where Kate didn't know and, frankly, wasn't certain if she really cared. Alone again, Kate dropped her hands to her side and leaned her forehead against the wall, the coolness of the plaster helping to calm her nerves. *Jacob*, she thought. *Why on earth did Becca have to bring up Jacob?*

It wasn't that she didn't think of Jacob. No, that wasn't true at all. But he had been just a toddler when he died. She pushed the memory from her mind, knowing that dwelling on it would only send her into a tailspin again. Twelve years had passed in a blink of an eye and yet the wound remained opened as if it had happened just yesterday.

With another deep breath, she reached for her black sweater and slipped it on. Downstairs, she could hear Daed call out for her. Although she dreaded arriving at the singing alone, she knew better than to argue with Daed. His mind was set. The only thing she could do was to clear her mind and focus on what needed to be done that evening.

The singing was being held at the Millers' house in the same room where the worship service had been held earlier that day. Once again, the benches were set up, but, unlike earlier that day, both the young men and the young women were in the room, gathered in groups as they visited before the singing began. Near the back of the room, a long table was set up with bowls of pretzels and chips as well as pitchers of water and lemonade.

As she stood in the doorway, Kate put on a brave face. Despite the pit that grew in her stomach, she forced herself to walk into the room, trying to look cheerful. She felt as if the small clusters of people stared at her. For a moment, she froze as she looked around and all their faces blurred together.

Were they whispering about her? If they were, it wasn't about whether her dress was wrinkled or her hem torn, the typical chit-chat and gossip among the different groups of young women. No. This time, they had something else to talk about, for the very fact that her *daed* had dropped her off at the youth singing and immediately left, without so much as a wave of his hand, warranted the stares and whispers, both imaginary and real.

They know, she told herself. Surely they knew she was to blame for the accident. Surely they knew she could have saved Ruth's life, if only she had spoken to her *daed* earlier, when she'd first discovered her brother's problem with whiskey . . . if only she hadn't kept David's secret.

Her eyes glazed over as she approached the refreshment table, trying to steady her hand as she reached for a glass of lemonade.

"You came!"

Kate spun around, lemonade splashing out of the cup and onto her hand. She laughed, a nervous laugh, and dabbed at her hand with the edge of her black apron. "Verna! You startled me!"

"I see that!" Verna smiled. "I'm glad you're here. I wondered if you'd show up."

"My *daed* insisted," Kate said. "I . . . I wasn't feeling very good about it."

Reaching out to take her hand, Verna tried to reassure her. "There's nothing to feel less than good about, Kate. Everyone has missed you."

Kate's eyes flickered across the room, too aware that others seemed to be watching her interaction with Verna. She wondered what they were thinking, feeling confident that they had whispered among each other after the accident . . . about David and Ruth . . . and about her role in what happened.

It wasn't my fault, she wanted to scream, to no one in particular. Most of all, she wanted to scream it to herself, because part of her wished she could begin to forgive herself. Deep down, however, she couldn't. She knew she was to blame. Likewise, she felt certain they knew it, too.

"Sit with us, then?"

Kate shook her head, lowering her eyes to stare at the floor. "Maybe in a spell," she offered as a concession. They both knew she wouldn't. Still, Kate saw how her presence pleased Verna and felt rewarded. It was just that by showing up, she'd used all of her courage for one day.

No sooner had Verna rejoined her friends when another person approached Kate from behind. This time, however, the voice that called out "Hey, Kate!" did not belong to a female friend.

At the sound of her name, she jumped.

"Care for some pretzels?"

Samuel stood beside her, a bowl of tiny pretzels in his hand. She could tell they were her favorite kind: the small home-baked pretzels that had been seasoned with Hidden Valley Ranch spices. The women often served bowls of these pretzels at the fellowship dinner following worship service, and Kate simply couldn't get enough of them. There was something tangy about the seasoning. Seeing Samuel holding out a bowl to her caught her off guard.

With a shaky hand, she took a pretzel and lowered her eyes. "*Danke*," she whispered.

He took a deep breath and glanced around the room. "It's right *gut* to see you tonight." He looked back at her and hesitated, just long enough for her to feel uncomfortable and lift her eyes. "Saw your *daed* dropped you off," he said.

She nodded.

"What changed your mind?"

Kate didn't want to confess that her *daed* forced her to attend. That might seem rude or, even worse, prideful. Some people might think that she felt she was better than them, too good to attend singings anymore. Of course, other people would know the real reason, which was the complete opposite: that the accident had made her a sinner who wanted to hide in shame.

So, rather than answer directly, Kate looked around. "Lot of people turned out for the singing, *ja*?"

He followed her example and glanced around the room. "Reckon so. Hadn't paid much attention before." She noticed that Ella Riehl stood on the other side of the room; more than once, she looked in his direction. Samuel did not return her meaningful looks. "Is your *daed* coming to fetch you later?"

Truth was that she didn't know. He never had been the one to bring her to and from singings, and it might not even occur to him to pick her up. With the early morning chores ahead of them, she highly doubted it. If anything, he was already home and in bed. "*Nee*," she said. "I don't think he is."

"Mayhaps I could take you home, then?"

The gasp came from someone else. Kate's eyes shifted toward the sound, but she could not see who had been responsible. She did, however, understand what it meant. Surely some in the community disapproved of her and therefore registered shock that an upstanding young man like Samuel Esh would be so kind to her. The last thing she wanted was to negatively affect his reputation.

She shook her head. "I . . . I prefer to walk, Samuel," she said, quickly adding, "but *danke* for asking."

At that, Samuel took another deep breath, his chest rising and then falling as he exhaled. For a moment, he kept silent and didn't respond, as if he were at a loss for words, but she could feel his eyes still studying her face. She tried to avoid making eye contact. It was impossible. When she finally relented and met his gaze, he tilted his head and raised his eyebrows. "All right then, Kate."

She thought that he would walk away, that the discussion was over. One rebuff was usually enough. She was wrong.

"If you don't mind," he said. "I shall walk with you, then."

Her mouth fell open at his announcement. While certainly very kind, she also knew it presented a rather undeniable inconvenience to him. If he walked her home, he'd have to walk back to get his horse and buggy. Clearly, he was intent on accompanying her. That was for sure and certain. Now, it was up to her whether she chose to make it more difficult for him.

"I reckon you could accompany me," she said slowly, her heart racing. The unexpected request to take her home had caught her off guard, and now his persistence was even more surprising. Would he really insist upon walking with her? "But I . . . I sure wouldn't want to walk past . . ."

He held up his hand. "We can walk the long way, Kate." And with that, it was settled. He gave her a quick smile before returning to his group of friends, only once looking over his shoulder to check on her before the singing started.

She sat on the periphery of a group of young women whom she'd attended school with years ago. Normally, theirs were familiar faces, as she saw them at worship service every other Sunday. But due to the winter weather and Kate's self-imposed isolation, she hadn't seen them in a long while.

"Why, hello there, Kate," a voice said in her ear.

She turned and saw Katie Ellen smiling at her. With her round glasses and cherubic face, Katie Ellen seemed genuinely pleased.

"Been a while since you came to a singing."

As if Katie Ellen needed to point that out, Kate thought. "I reckon so," she mumbled.

"How's the family been?"

"As *gut* as can be expected." It was the only reply that Kate could muster.

"And your *bruder*?" Katie Ellen hesitated. "David?"

At the sound of her brother's name, Kate caught her breath. She knew the questions would come. Certainly people were curious. Why wouldn't they be? After all, it was David who caused the accident. Of course, she had come to realize that she shouldered as much of the blame as David did . . . perhaps more. But talking about any of this directly with Katie Ellen was impossible.

"He's getting along better, I reckon." Noticing that several other young women shifted their attention toward what she said, Kate lowered her eyes. "Still can't walk and doesn't talk much."

Katie Ellen clicked her tongue. Tsk-tsk. It wasn't a judgmental gesture. No, it was one of pity.

That reaction was how Kate felt most of the time. Every day, she watched David sitting in the borrowed wheelchair, gazing out the window at the fields that he would never plow. The farm, once intended to be his to work and raise a family on, now remained unclaimed for the future. Who would take over and raise the crops and tend to the cows? Her older brother had married years ago. The plan had always been that David would be the one.

"And . . . have you heard how Ruth's family is doing?" Kate hated asking the question but knew it was appropriate. After all that the *g'may* had been through, Ruth's family deserved that respect.

Katie Ellen took a deep breath before she answered. "Her *maem* stopped by the other day. Guess she's doing all right. She didn't say nothing about Ruth."

Kate wasn't surprised by Katie Ellen's remarks. To lament the passing of a person was to question God. Many Amish families never spoke about people who passed away. They certainly did not grieve publicly.

Thankfully, the *vorsinger* began the first song at that very moment, singing the first few notes as an indication that it was time for the rest of the youth group to join in. Kate tried to pay attention to the words, as it was a faster song than what was typically sung during worship service but still expressed a tribute to God and His love for the righteous.

While her lips moved, her mind wandered, contemplating that word: righteous.

Ever since the accident, she had questioned the true meaning of that word. Was it possible for her to be righteous? For anyone? She often wondered if, once fallen, she would be able to ever achieve the moral standards that God expected of His people and the bishop expected of his *g'may*. She knew, of course, that no person could ever achieve perfection. People were destined to sin. Perfection had been saved for only one person: Jesus, the Son of God. Still, her failures ran too deep and worry had kept her awake at night more often than not, especially when she remembered all the times she contemplated telling her parents about David's drinking.

His pleading had convinced her otherwise.

Now, because she had listened to him and said nothing to her parents about the hidden bottle of whiskey she'd found behind the mule shed, a cloud of guilt hung over her head. Even worse, he spent his days in a wheelchair and Ruth spent hers six feet under the ground, waiting for the Second Coming of Jesus.

"You ready to leave, then?"

Kate looked up, her thoughts broken by Samuel's soft words in her ear. She glanced around, noticing that she stood alone. Being so absorbed in her own tragic thoughts was a social hazard, that was for sure and certain. She hadn't even noticed that the singing group had taken a break and dispersed to visit with one another. Surely Samuel had noticed Kate standing alone, oblivious, when he decided to approach her.

"The singing isn't over."

He shrugged, pushing his hands into his front pockets. "*Nee*, it isn't. But mayhaps you've had enough?"

She couldn't control the look of gratitude that washed over her face. She felt relieved to have an excuse to escape the singing, so without any hesitation she nodded her head.

"I thought so."

Slipping through the open door, Samuel guided her through the darkness down the lane. When she paused as he passed the long line of buggies parked along the fence, he turned and she sensed, rather than saw, his smile.

"Your buggy?" she asked.

"You said you wanted to walk."

"But then you'd have to walk back."

This time, he laughed. "Don't you worry about me none, Kate Zook. I'd much rather spend the extra time walking beside you anyway."

The darkness hid the color that rushed to her cheeks. For that, she was grateful.

During the first few minutes, they walked in silence. She listened to the noise of their shoes on the roads, the slight crunching of the gravel beneath their soles. It made a musical rhythm and, once again, she found herself counting the notes of the song: *one, two, three, four.* She shivered once and buttoned her jacket so that it kept her throat warm.

"You cold, then?"

She liked the way he talked. He seemed to read her mind, and when he asked a question, there was a raised inflection on the final word. His deep voice matched his tall, broad-shouldered physique. Many of the Amish young men were tall and skinny. Not Samuel Esh.

Before the accident, when Kate had attended the singings, she hadn't given Samuel Esh much thought. After all, he was closer in age to her older brother, Thomas. Additionally, every one had known that Samuel was escorting Ella Riehl home from singings, and most in the *g'may* suspected the courtship would end in marriage. Most courtships remained secret until the bishop announced a couple's wedding banns at a worship service in October, but it wasn't always easy to keep things under wraps.

Of course, back in those days, before the accident, she'd focused her attention more on her girlfriends. At that time, they were more important to her than any of the young men. But time stood still for no one. Slowly, each of her friends paired off with a young man, while she did not. She never thought twice about it. Not really.

As she walked, however, Kate realized that it was happening to her: for the first time, a young man was escorting her home from a singing. She had to admit, of all the young men in the *g'may*, Samuel Esh was the last person she'd thought would ask to walk her home. His age and work ethic clearly indicated that he was ready to settle down. She wondered what happened between him and Ella. Being older than Kate, Ella would have made him a right *gut* wife!

Besides, Kate thought, Ella had surely never sinned . . . not like she had.

"Seems like the weather is changing," he said. "A bit warmer. Days are longer, too, now that we're on slow time. I like slow time better."

Kate realized that she'd neglected to answer him regarding being cold. If she remained unresponsive to his last comment, she risked him thinking she was rude. "*Ja*, me, too," she said. "Don't have to get up so early on Sundays for worship."

He laughed, his breath forming a small cloud in the chilly air.

"I never understood why the bishops don't change the worship time when the clocks move back!"

Despite taking the long way, it only took fifteen minutes to walk her home. Along the way, she listened to Samuel talk about working his *daed*'s farm and how they were preparing the fields for the spring planting. As the time passed, she felt increasingly comfortable around him and even enjoyed his story about finding an Indian arrowhead in the field.

"Can you imagine? That farm's been in our family for over a hundred years! I wonder how many times people overlooked that stone!"

"People don't often pay attention to the little things," she responded. "Lucky for you that they didn't."

He laughed again. "Why, I never thought of it that way!"

Once they arrived at the mailbox, Samuel seemed to walk a little slower. She wondered if he slowed his pace intentionally. "I feel bad you have to walk back alone."

"Why, I have an idea!" He seemed excited and stood facing her in the darkness. Even though it was dark, she could sense that he was smiling. "You could walk back with me! And then I'd bring you home in the buggy!"

She couldn't help herself from laughing. "Oh, that would be silly now, wouldn't it?"

He nudged her gently with his shoulder. "I'm teasing you, Kate." He leaned down and, with a lowered voice, added, "Although I will confess that if you said yes, I wouldn't have been disappointed!"

She blushed, glad for the second time that evening that the darkness hid her reaction.

"You take care now, Kate Zook." He reached out a hand and gently touched her arm. She felt a tingle of warmth and stepped back. He chuckled, so soft that she almost didn't hear him. "And I'll be seeing you around, then."

She nodded, uncertain whether he could see. "*Danke*, Samuel," she said.

With his hands thrust into his pockets, he walked backward for a few steps before turning around. She noticed that he picked up his pace, walking faster and taking the longer route, the route that bypassed the broken buggy on the side of the road. Something about that decision warmed her heart, and as she walked into the house, she realized how relieved that choice made her. *Finally*, she thought. *Someone who understands . . .*

CHAPTER SIX

The following Saturday, she noticed it was missing right away.

With temperatures climbing into the midfifties during the week, the snow had completely given way to soggy fields and dull brown grass with hints of green. Although the trees remained bare, their gray limbs stretched toward the blue sky. The activity of the birds increased as they flew from branch to branch, chirping and singing. As she walked to her *aendi*'s house to help with the *boppli*, the fence rail remained broken as always. But the buggy was now missing.

Despite immediately realizing that something was amiss, it took her a moment to recognize the empty place where the buggy's twisted frame had lingered, a constant reminder of David's poor decision making and her sin in hiding his secret. It was gone.

She stopped walking and stared, blinking several times in disbelief. No one had spoken about moving the wreckage. Daed certainly never mentioned it. In fact, during the prior week, he'd spent most of his time in the fields, tilling the soil and then spreading manure to fertilize it in preparation for the planting of corn seed. Kate knew this because she had worked alongside him.

She felt a welcome lightness inside her chest. The buggy was gone. Simply . . . gone! Since it had been situated on private property, the local law enforcement refused to remove it. In fact, they hadn't been called until well after David reached the hospital and Ruth was already being tended to by the funeral director. The bishop had stepped forward, refusing to allow the police to intervene, stating that it was merely an accident—something to be dealt with by the family and church.

No one had ever tested David's blood alcohol level. No one had attempted to prove that he had been intoxicated. In fact, the question of what caused the accident never was discussed. No one knew about the involvement of alcohol.

Only Kate knew. Well, and David knew, of course. If Daed suspected it, he never said. Kate did notice that in the days after the accident, an empty whiskey bottle had appeared in the rubbish bin. Certainly Daed had retrieved it from the wreckage. But no one ever spoke of David's misconduct in causing the accident. *Less said, soonest mended*, Maem often said. Unfortunately, in this situation, only saying more, not less, could have brought mending and healing.

So without any criminal charges filed, the buggy was not considered evidence. And so it had sat there, on private property, throughout the long winter. The owner of the field, Amos Lapp, hadn't bothered to fix the fence or remove the buggy's remains because it bordered along the road near the Zooks, far back on his own property.

Of course, with so much snow and ice, there had been weeks where the buggy simply could not be removed. But now, now that the snow had melted, someone had finally addressed the constant reminder of that night.

It was gone.

Curious, she walked the rest of the way with her head spinning, realizing that her dozens of questions would likely never get answered. When had it disappeared? It could have been anytime during the week. Who had removed it? Was it Amos Lapp or Daed? Perhaps it was Ruth's family, tired of avoiding that road in their travels?

It wasn't until later that afternoon that she managed to broach the subject with her *maem*. David was sitting on the porch, a lap blanket over his useless legs as, at Maem's request, he took in the afternoon sun before the supper hour. Kate set the table, making certain to remove one chair as usual to make room for David's wheelchair.

"Noticed something different today," she started, setting the chair in the corner by the cupboard.

"Oh *ja*?" Maem barely looked up from where she stood at the counter, cutting into a fresh loaf of bread. She set the slices on a plate and handed it to Kate to put on the table. "And what was that, then?"

"The buggy," Kate said softly. Her eyes flickered toward David, hoping that he couldn't overhear her. Since he continued staring out into the distance, she presumed he could not. Returning her attention to her *maem*, she lowered her voice. "It's gone."

For a moment, Maem did not reply. She pursed her lips and inhaled deeply. The silence lingered, just long enough to tell Kate what she wanted to know: Maem knew nothing about the removal of the buggy. Yet, from the expression on her face, her *maem* clearly felt relief. The same thing Kate had experienced earlier. With the visual reminder finally gone, perhaps some healing might begin.

"Wasn't Daed then, I reckon," Kate said as a way of asking the unspoken question that had lingered on her mind all day, ever since she first walked past the empty spot earlier that morning.

"*Nee*."

"Then who?"

Maem shrugged her shoulders in a way that indicated sorrow rather than lack of interest. "Surely the bishop arranged it." She turned her back to Kate and poured some homemade applesauce into a large bowl. "Won't hurt anyone to have it gone," she said under her breath. Kate thought she heard her mother whisper "finally," but she couldn't be certain.

No one spoke further about the buggy, although Kate suspected Maem mentioned it to Daed in the privacy of the washroom. He seemed even more withdrawn than usual during supper, glancing occasionally at David with a look in his eyes that spoke of sorrow and disappointment. David kept his eyes on his plate, never once looking up at anyone seated around the table.

"Saw Samuel Esh today," Daed said, glancing in Kate's direction. The announcement was clearly important, so everyone stopped eating and looked up. "Stopped by to visit with David."

Silence.

Kate felt compelled to respond since everyone stared at her. "Did he now?" She looked at her brother. "That sure was nice of Samuel to visit you, David." At the mention of Samuel's name, her heart beat rapidly and she hoped that her cheeks didn't take on obvious color.

David grunted, but said nothing.

"I sure hope you were more pleasant than that when he came calling," Maem said tersely.

Kate could tell when her mother was annoyed. Clearly, this was one of those times. Her usual way was to speak in a soft tone and never raise her voice to her children. However, that seemed to be changing as of late. Her even temperament disappeared more frequently, especially in the past two weeks.

David didn't respond but scowled at his *maem* for the reproach.

"I thought I heard a buggy earlier," Maem said, directing her statement back at Daed.

"Fine young man, that Esh boy."

If Kate hadn't blushed before, she knew her cheeks bloomed pink at that last statement.

"Was driving by and stopped in to see how David was doing." Daed nodded his head. "Been a while since any of the young men have come around. Wondered about that myself."

No one needed to remind Daed that David had all but chased away any visitors. His negative moods didn't create a warm, inviting atmosphere, that was for sure and certain. There had been a flood of visitors after the accident, especially in the days immediately following David's return from the hospital. He'd turned away every one of them, choosing to stay in his dark room and wallow in his misery rather than socialize. It didn't take long for the visits to stop.

"We were outside," Daed continued, ignoring David and concentrating on Kate. "He asked if you were home."

Kate raised her eyebrows, ignoring the giggles that escaped from Becca's mouth. "Me?" She glanced at her *maem* and noticed that she was still eating. Clearly she already knew whatever Daed was going to say. "Whatever for?"

"He your boyfriend, Kate?"

"*Nee*!" Kate frowned as she scowled at Becca who sat opposite her at the table. But from the grin on Becca's face, she clearly did not believe her older sister.

"A youth group is taking a ride over to the park on Stumptown Road to try their hand at fishing. Asked if you might want to join them."

Once again, Kate found herself speechless. First the rides home on the previous two Saturdays after she worked at Susan's house and then he'd walked her home from the singing last week. Now fishing? She didn't know this young man, had barely exchanged a dozen words with him in the past five years and now, suddenly, he seemed to be everywhere.

"Too cold to go fishing," she said quickly. "Besides, I'm needed here." She couldn't believe that she needed to point that out to her parents. After all, without her help, who would assist Maem with David on Sunday afternoon?

"Nonsense." Daed shook his head. There was a determined look on his face, one that worried Kate. "Time you get out and about, Kate. He'll be here to fetch you at one o'clock."

"At one?" Becca groaned. "Means more barn chores for me, then," Becca pouted, the grin quickly disappearing from her face as she slapped her hand against her forehead. "Great."

Maem shook her head, disapproving of Becca's reaction.

"I don't like the cold," Kate said softly.

Daed clenched his teeth. "You'll be going, Kate. Won't be having two of my *kinner* sitting around moping about the past!"

David snapped to attention, clearly aware that he was the other *kinner* being referenced by Daed. "I wouldn't be moping if someone had gotten in the buggy and driven it!"

"Oh hush, boy!"

Kate bit her lip and stared down at her hands, folded neatly on her lap. She didn't need to look at her *daed* to know that his eyes flashed with anger, the extent of his emotions mirrored by the harshness of his voice.

"It's time to get on with your own life and let Kate get on with hers!"

"Is that what you told Jacob?" David snapped, his eyes narrow and glaring at his *daed*.

Maem gasped, her hand lifting to cover her mouth as she fought the tears that immediately flooded her eyes.

"Oh wait, you couldn't tell him that because he died, didn't he?" He rolled his eyes to look at Kate. "And whose fault was that, I wonder?"

Daed pounded his closed fist against the tabletop, the plates rattled, and Becca's water glass fell over. She hurried to right it, dabbing at the puddle of water on the table with the edge of her dirty apron. "I'll have no more of that talk!" He pointed a finger at his son. "No more of that out of your mouth, David."

Kate trembled, her appetite vanished, and her hands shook so hard that she lowered them to her lap. Twelve years may have passed, but the pain was still fresh. She blinked her eyes rapidly, willing herself to remain strong. David's harsh reminder stung and she wished that she could just stand up, leave the table, and cry in peace.

She caught Becca steal a glance at her. Kate averted her eyes, but not before she saw the questioning look on her youngest sister's face. Becca was the only one who hadn't been born yet when Jacob passed away. Of course, Miriam had been just a small baby, so she clearly didn't remember that difficult year. No one spoke about it, so only whispers of comments from other people had informed her younger sisters about that summer day that ended in tragedy.

Kate pushed the memory as far away as possible. There was no use rehashing it. *Move on*, she thought, repeating Maem's words.

For the rest of the meal, everyone ate in silence. David picked at his plate, a scowl on his face. Kate's appetite was gone, but she knew better than to waste food. Forcing herself to finish her plate, she escaped into her mind, repeating the Lord's Prayer three times as a way to calm down.

Oh, she knew David felt pain. His anger was a mask for his true feelings of loss and grief. That didn't excuse his horrible words to her, however. After all, words hurt. Still, she reminded herself, not for the first time, that the pain she felt from his verbal abuse could not compare to David's memory of waking up in the hospital with a severed spine and a broken arm to hear the news that his girlfriend was dead. If alcoholism was truly a disease, Kate knew David had been sick with it, which made it hard to blame him. She had not suffered from a disease. No, she'd simply failed to speak up, and she felt the burden of guilt for it.

After the family finished the meal and the after-prayer was said, Daed pushed back his plate and left the table. Moments later, she heard him walking across the front porch, his footsteps heavy on the stairs as he disappeared in the direction of the barn.

Kate quickly hurried to clean the dishes while her younger sisters cleared the table. Gone were the days of laughing after supper, playing board games or going for evening walks. Daed's propensity toward perpetual anger seemed to create a negative energy in the house, even worse than David's sulking attitude.

Kate busied herself in washing the dishes, wondering how her mother managed to hold everything together. Besides coping with David and the moodiness that accompanied his permanent handicap, she was forced to deal with Daed's constant irritability as well. While Kate knew that God gave people what they could handle, she often prayed that He'd give her mother just a little less once in a while.

CHAPTER SEVEN

The sound of the buggy pulling into the lane interrupted Kate's thoughts as she sat on the sofa, reading her Bible. The worn leather cover felt smooth and familiar to her hands. In Kate's eyes, there was nothing better to do on a Sunday afternoon than read the book of Psalms. The pages were marked with crocheted bookmarks and slips of paper that she had placed there as a way to remember her favorite passages.

Today, however, she would have to put away her Bible and forego reading her favorite Psalms. When the horse's hooves stopped and she heard the not-so-familiar sound of Daed greeting a visitor, Kate sighed. She shut the Bible and set it on the end table, her eyes glancing at the clock as her heart pounded. With impeccable punctuality, Samuel arrived at exactly one o'clock.

Kate glanced at her *maem*, who, thankfully, did not look back. Kate knew that any sideways glances or raised eyebrows would have sent her scurrying upstairs and into her bedroom. She did not want to go with Samuel to the youth gathering. She wasn't ready yet. Unfortunately, arguing with Daed was not an option.

When he knocked at the door, Kate stood up. She brushed at the front of her navy-blue dress before sighing, just once more, and then walking to the door.

He greeted her with a smile, his eyes bright and sparkly from beneath the shadow of his straw hat. "You ready for some fishing, then?"

She responded with a simple nod and joined him on the porch. "I don't have any gear or nothing." She wasn't certain why she said that; it wasn't as though he would refuse to take her. She immediately felt embarrassed and stared at the door handle.

"No matter," he said, and gestured toward the buggy. She noticed the top of two fishing poles sticking out of the back window. "I brought plenty for both of us, I'm sure."

If he sensed her hesitation, he made no indication. Instead, he gave her a lopsided grin before he walked toward his buggy. The brown mare stood at the hitching post, rubbing her nose against the metal bar. Samuel untied the lead rope and waited until Kate placed her foot on the iron step and climbed inside the buggy. Then he joined her, careful not to jiggle the buggy when he did.

"Sure do love this time of year." At the end of her lane, he paused the horse, looking both ways before directing the mare to turn left. "I reckon spring is my favorite season. What about you, Kate?"

She hesitated. She wasn't used to engaging in such conversation. At home, most of the conversation focused on chores or things that happened within the community. With her friends, when she used to go out with them, most of their conversation focused on their families and any gossip. Personal questions soliciting her opinion didn't seem to pop up too often.

"Well," she began, "there is magic in every season. I don't think I have a favorite. Each season has something special about it. To pick one over the others? Why, I don't think it would be fair to the rest."

He glanced at her, a smile on his face. "Why, that's the most tenderhearted response anyone could have given!"

She blushed.

He cleared his throat and shifted the reins in his hands. "Was sorry to have missed seeing you yesterday when I stopped by to visit David."

The sudden change of the conversation startled her. Had he sensed her discomfort at his compliment? "That was right nice of you to visit him. I'm sure he appreciated it."

"Seems a bit improved."

Kate frowned. Had Samuel visited David before yesterday? If he had, she knew nothing about it. She wanted to ask, but felt awkward prying into his private business. Kate turned her head to look out the window. She wondered why Samuel had decided to visit at all. Everyone knew he was closer in age to Thomas than David.

As if reading her mind, Samuel answered the question for her. "Last time I saw him was after the funeral," he explained. "Seems so long ago, *ja?*"

Kate shut her eyes. She didn't want to think about the funeral. The haunting memory of the sorrowful faces as the people single-filed past the simple pine coffin, the hinged lid folded back so that only Ruth's face was exposed, stayed with her. And then the scene at the graveyard . . .

She shook her head, as if to wipe the memory away before she turned back to Samuel. "That was nice to stop by to see him," she managed to say, forcing a smile despite the urge she felt to ask him to bring her home. She knew that her *daed* spoke the truth when he'd insisted it was time for her to get out and return to socializing with the other youth in the *g'may*.

Samuel stared at her, a strange look on his face. She wondered what he was thinking, but she did not ask.

He guided the horse and buggy down the road, taking a deep breath. "Sure am glad you came along."

She didn't know how to respond.

"Much nicer to have some company."

She wasn't certain that she was great company. She didn't know what to say; she couldn't exactly say aloud that she hadn't wanted to join him, anyway. "*Danke* for asking me along," she said, trying to remember her manners.

He smiled. "I was driving by your *daed*'s farm and thought to myself, 'Now, wouldn't it be nice to see if Kate Zook might want to accompany me when I go fishing?' It's so much nicer to have someone to talk to besides myself. Doing too much of that lately. One-sided conversations are boring after a while."

She wondered if he was hinting that he no longer saw Ella Riehl. She had already figured that he had ended his courtship with Ella. After all, he had walked home with her, not Ella, after the singing. While Kate initially wondered when he had broken it off from Ella, she now had an even bigger question: Why? She wished she could ask someone, perhaps Verna or Katie Ellen, but she didn't feel that was appropriate. Time would tell, she told herself.

When the buggy stopped alongside the river, Kate took a moment to enjoy the view. Hints of fresh green growth were bringing color to the brown grass scattered along the riverbank. With the sun shining in the sky, it felt like spring, even if it did not look like it. Kate thought she saw the tops of daffodils poking through the dirt on the other side of the riverbank. A robin swooped down from the bare trees, its red breast proud and round as it dipped its beak into the dirt, most likely looking for a worm. Kate wondered if it was a female or male. It was too far away for her to identify properly.

"You coming?"

She returned her attention to the moment. While she'd been daydreaming, he'd retrieved the fishing gear and now held it in his hands, waiting for her to join him.

Several other Amish youths sat around a picnic table just a few yards away from the parking lot. Kate recognized all of them, including Samuel's brother, John, and lifted her hand to greet them. One of the young women bounced up and hurried over to Kate, reaching out to grasp her hand.

"I'm so glad you came, Kate!"

Kate smiled in response. It was always a pleasure to see Esther, although seeing her did bring back memories of that fateful night. If Kate hadn't been at her house that night, requiring David to come and pick her up, perhaps the whole accident never would have happened.

"Come sit over here while the boys get their rods ready."

"Esther!" One of the young men looked up from his tackle box, a surprised look on his face. "Aren't you planning on fishing at all, then?"

"Oh, John! You know I'm squeamish about those squiggly worms!" Laughing, Esther looked back at Kate. "I'd rather just enjoy the sun, wouldn't you?"

In truth, Kate didn't mind the worms. When she was younger, she'd always enjoyed fishing with her older brother. Back in those days, sometimes David joined them, too. One summer, Thomas even taught her how to hook the worm just right so that it wouldn't fall off in the current. But she didn't want to seem too proud by saying that.

"Sitting in the sun is rather nice," Kate admitted.

Samuel didn't seem to mind that she joined the other young women at the picnic table. He carried his rod and tackle box down to the stream, joining two other young men who already stood there, lines in the water, sun on their backs.

"Been quite a winter," Esther said. "Heard your *daed*'s barn roof collapsed from the snow." She directed the comment to a young woman, Sylvia Yoder, sitting on the other side of the table.

"*Ja*, it sure did."

This was news to Kate! She hadn't heard about damage to the Yoders' barn. Although they lived in the same church district, their farm was farther away. She wondered when it happened but felt too embarrassed to ask. How could she not have known about this? After all, Sylvia's *onkel*'s family lived next to the Zooks' farm!

"How about you, Kate?" Esther shifted her weight, facing Kate directly. "It's been a rough winter for your family, I know. Is David getting any better?"

And there it was. The question that lingered over everyone's head, but until now remained unasked. The question that Kate dreaded. The reason she avoided attending youth gatherings. The reminder that she could have prevented that tragedy from ever happening.

"I . . . I really prefer not to talk about it," she whispered.

Placing her hand on Kate's arm, Esther tried to reassure her. "It's all right to talk about it," she said. "We all pray for David every night in my family. We also pray for your family as well as Ruth's."

"It was an accident," Sylvia added solemnly. "But it was also God's will."

Kate hesitated. She grew weary of hearing the same rhetoric about accidents and will. *If the members of the community only knew the truth*, she thought. God's will or Satan's hand? The question haunted her daily, especially when she considered her role. Why had she listened to David? Why hadn't she told Daed? Why had she insisted upon walking home when she realized that David was drunk? And why hadn't she insisted that Ruth come with her?

"Mayhaps I will try my hand at fishing after all," she said as she stood up and then hurried down to the riverbank.

Samuel gave her a lopsided grin when she joined him. "Changed your mind, then?" He handed her his pole and took a step back, giving her room to stand closer to the edge of the water. "Thatta girl!"

His praise startled her. She felt a blush creep onto her cheeks. The rod felt stiff and unfamiliar in her hands. It had been years since she last fished with Thomas. Once he'd married Linda, his focus shifted to his work and family, which now also consisted of one *boppli*, a little boy named Stephen.

She jiggled the rod, just a touch. Within minutes, the line grew taut and the end of the rod tipped ever so slightly.

"Hey now!" Samuel exclaimed. "I think you caught something!"

He seemed genuinely pleased and that, too, caused her to blush. Redirecting her attention to the fishing rod, she carefully reeled in the line, occasionally jerking the rod backward so that the hook would stay in the fish's mouth. When it broke the water and splashed on the surface, Esther and Sylvia joined them, squealing in delight at the excitement of the first catch of the day.

"Stream trout," Samuel announced as he reached for the line to lift the fish out of the water. "Big one at that, too!" He beamed at Kate. "You're a natural!"

"No better than anyone else with a worm on a hook, I reckon." Still, she found herself enjoying the warmth of his compliments as well as the pride in his eyes.

"Make for a nice supper!"

"You keep him." Kate felt it was only fair since she used his gear and his bait.

Samuel quickly pulled the fish from the hook and placed it in a red cooler. "Mayhaps you'll catch enough for both families, ain't so?"

"Mayhaps," she responded, wondering why she felt that increasingly familiar flutter inside of her chest when he grinned at her.

She watched as he hooked the worm onto the line and held her tongue when she wanted to tell him how to do it properly. To her relief, he managed to double hook the worm properly, just the way Thomas had taught her so many years ago. She knew it wouldn't do to correct him and was pleased that she didn't have to.

"There you go," he said, handing her the rod. "Let's see how you cast, then!"

When she cast out the line, he laughed and placed his hand on her shoulder. "My, my! Seems you been fishing before, ain't so?"

She nodded.

"I used to fish with your *bruder* Thomas."

His announcement surprised Kate. "Did you now?"

He nodded his head. "I reckon he's the one that taught you?"

"*Ja.*" She felt the tension loosen in her body, even when he didn't remove his hand from her shoulder. The weight of it felt heavy but comforting at the same time. The gentleness of his touch soothed her raw nerves. It had been a long time since she felt such genuine kindness from someone. "Thomas was a good fisherman."

"That he was," Samuel admitted, letting his hand drop from her shoulder. "Reckon he still is but for want of time."

Time. The word rang in her head. After Ruth's funeral, Kate remembered thinking about time and how unpredictable it was. She often lay awake at night, thinking about Ruth's too-short life. Just the idea of a life cut short made Kate realize how powerless they were in the shadow of God's plan. Each day needed to be lived and spent honoring God in thought, prayer, and deed.

During Ruth's funeral service, the bishop had made a point of specifically preaching about the value of time. He'd proclaimed that everyone should be thankful and praise God for the time shared with each other. He never came right out and said that Ruth was too young to die such an unfortunate death. To do so would be to question God's will. And that would be very non-Amish.

Kate, however, had thought it.

"I reckon we all want for time to have fun," she finally said. "But too much time invested in fun is not a good thing."

He nodded his head, acknowledging the wisdom of her words. "This is true, Kate Zook." He reached for his own fishing pole, unhooking the J-shaped hook from the line. "But doing nothing fun isn't a good thing either now, is it?" He knelt down and began fingering through the dirt in the Styrofoam cup at his feet until he pulled out a long earthworm. He wrapped it around and through the hook twice, this time with more confidence, before positioning himself to cast the line into the stream.

She watched him, her curiosity piqued as he swung the line back and, with precise expertise, snapped the pole toward the water, releasing the line at exactly the right moment so that it sailed over hers. It landed in the center of the stream.

"Take fishing, for example," Samuel said casually. He spread his feet and faced the water. "It's relaxing and fun." He glanced at her and smiled. "At least to me, anyway." He returned his attention to the line. "Still, if I'm able to catch enough food to feed my family, well . . . it's work, too, I reckon. After six long days of helping my *daed* with the farm chores and field work, it's nice to take a little break and do something different. Opens my heart and soul to reflect on things."

"What kinds of things?" Her voice sounded small as she asked the question.

He glanced at her once again. "Well, things about life and God and the future."

The future? The future was ordained already, the journey already mapped out in a book written and read by God alone. For years, Kate had been told that God had a plan for her future that was already written in that book. It made accepting tragedy easier to handle, that was for sure and certain.

"Being out here with nature and friends," Samuel continued. "It sure makes the days of hard work seem more worthwhile, don't you think?"

She had never looked at it that way. Rewards for hard work?

"You look perplexed, Kate."

She looked at him, not wanting to question what he said but curious to learn more about his personal philosophy. "That's just a different perspective from what I'm used to, I reckon."

"Different in a good or bad way?"

She smiled, not certain how to respond. There was something refreshing about Samuel Esh. His positive energy made her feel lighter than she had in recent months. Or maybe it was the fresh air and the fact that she was doing something away from her family, the farm, and work. "I'm not sure yet."

"Well, you let me know when you figure it out, *ja*?" He winked and laughed, returning his attention to the fishing rod as it began to jiggle. "Look at that! Another bite! It's a banner day!" he shouted, reeling in the line.

By the time the sun began dipping in the sky, an indication that it was time to start heading home for late-afternoon chores, there was enough fish for everyone to take home at least two for their families. Samuel made certain to clean and wrap the fish in newspaper, storing both his and Kate's in the red cooler he'd brought along just for that purpose.

"Can't stand fish smell in the buggy," he commented as he packed the fish inside of it. He was placing the cooler in the back of the buggy when he lifted out a small cardboard box. "Almost forgot, Kate. Maem sent along some horseradish roots for your *maem*."

Kate frowned. "I just picked up roots the other week, ain't so?"

He shrugged. "Guess she had more. Knows how much your *maem* likes to garden."

Kate smiled, knowing her *maem* would be pleased. On that little plot of land, Maem cultivated her perennials as well herbs for both food and medicinal purposes. Kate often wondered if it just wasn't her way to escape for a while, to reflect in a place that *kinner* would not interrupt her while she spoke to God. Or perhaps it was her way to mourn the loss of Jacob's life through the cultivation and nurturing of plants. After all, she'd started her garden just after Jacob died.

Kate never asked her *maem* for details or reasons, respecting the fact that whatever Maem sought in that garden was special to her and certainly not any business of the rest of the family. Kate understood Maem's need for a respite. She often longed for one, herself.

After loading the fishing equipment, Samuel helped Kate into the buggy before he untied the horse from the hitching post. He smiled at her as he climbed inside, sitting beside her on the seat. "Ready?"

She nodded. "*Ja*, ready."

Despite the late hour, he took the longer route home. She didn't question his motives as she listened to him tell her stories about his family, mostly focusing on Joshua's antics.

"What about your family? Any fun stories?" he asked.

Kate shrugged. "Not lately, that's for sure and certain."

He remained silent, his eyes on the road ahead. The horse trotted in front of the buggy, its tail swishing back and forth, oblivious to the serious nature of the conversation in the buggy it pulled. Finally, Samuel looked at her. "Wallowing in the past is not honoring God," he said, a serious expression on his face. "Mayhaps it's time to move forward, ain't so?"

What's done is done . . .

"Accidents happen, Kate. God's plan intended for Ruth's death and for David's injury."

Best to move on . . .

"There's no reason that you can't find fun again."

She wished she felt comfortable telling Samuel the entire story. Telling him about that night and David's drinking. Confessing to her own sins of inaction, which might have saved Ruth's life. How many nights did she lay awake in bed, trying to understand God's plan and how she, Kate Zook, had failed him? Those hours, lying in her bed and staring at the ceiling, were her herb garden, her place of retreat to contemplate the past and worry about the future.

"Just takes time, I reckon," she said meekly. "It's only been four months."

"Five months now that it's April," he corrected. "And then some."

She raised an eyebrow, curious that Samuel remembered the timing of the accident so well. "Five months," she repeated.

"So," he said, his tone suddenly jovial once again as he returned his attention to the road, lifting his hand to wave at a buggy that passed by, headed in the opposite direction. "Tell me something funny about your family, then!"

She struggled for a few long seconds, trying to think of anything to say. The last thing she wanted was for Samuel to think she was dull and morose, even if her life had felt that way recently. "Well," she began slowly, searching her memory. "My youngest *schwester*, Becca . . . she sounds an awful lot like your *bruder* Joshua."

Samuel grinned. "How so?"

Focusing her thoughts on Becca suddenly made it much easier to talk to Samuel. Slowly at first, Kate began to tell him stories about Becca and her quirky, sassy ways. When he laughed at all of the right places in her stories, she felt encouraged and continued talking. Before she knew it, she was laughing with him and forgetting about the tragedy that lingered over her family home.

"Why, I'm surprised I haven't heard Joshua talking about your *schwester*," Samuel laughed. "They sound like two peas in a pod. What about your other *schwester*?"

"Miriam?" Kate didn't know what to say about her. "She's quiet and more reserved. More proper, I reckon. But she *is* older."

"Like you, then?"

Kate blushed. She didn't know how to respond. If she said yes, he might think she was boastful. If she said no, he'd think she was not proper. She remained silent instead.

Obviously noticing her discomfort, he laughed and nudged her gently with his elbow. "Aw, Kate," he teased. "You don't have to answer. I didn't mean to make you uncomfortable."

She looked out the window, hoping he didn't see her cheeks.

He chuckled under his breath, but not in a malicious way. She wanted to smile. His happy-go-lucky perspective felt contagious. She just had trouble letting go of her inhibitions. During her lifetime, she had never been afforded the luxury of gentle teasing and pleasant compliments. It took some getting used to; that was for sure and certain.

All too soon, the mailbox at the end of the lane for the Zooks' farm appeared. All of the relaxation that she felt began to vanish as she wondered what might await her inside the house. She steeled herself for the unexpected. After a day of socializing and laughing, Kate knew that she was destined to encounter unpleasantness from David.

He stopped the buggy just near the corner of the barn and stepped on the brake. Smiling, he hurried out of the open door of his buggy and reached out his hand to help Kate climb down. "Sure was fun, Kate," he said as she stood before him.

"*Danke* for asking me, Samuel," she said, avoiding his eyes. She didn't want him to see the sorrow she felt, knowing that such a fun day would be followed by a long week of hard labor, terse comments, and an angry environment. With Miriam and Becca finishing up the last weeks of school before summer vacation, there would be no buffers to protect Kate from David's barrage of negative attention.

"Don't forget your fish," he reminded her as he went to the back of the buggy and dug through the cooler. Extracting three fish, the individual wrapping paper soggy, he frowned. "Should I carry them inside for you so you don't get fish smell on your hands?"

She smiled, touched at his generous offer but not wanting to subject him to whatever awaited her inside the house. "That's OK. I'll get fish smell on my hands cooking them, ain't so?"

He laughed, handing her the fish. "I reckon you sure do have a point there! Can't cook fish without handling them."

Taking the fish, she started to walk to the house, too aware that he was watching her. At the porch steps, she glanced over her shoulder, not too surprised to see that he lingered by the side of his buggy.

"You have yourself a great week, Kate Zook!" he called out, his finger on the brim of his hat and a twinkle in his eyes.

Blushing, she dipped her head and ran into the house, her heart beating and pulse racing. She leaned against the door, smiling to herself as she listened to the sound of his horse pulling the buggy down the driveway and toward the road. For just one long second, she clung to that feeling, as if suspended in air, floating in happiness.

"Kate? You back already?" Maem called from the kitchen. "Daed'll be needing your help, then."

With a deep breath, she shut her eyes and said good-bye to the glow of joy that she felt. *Reality*, she thought. *There is no escape from it.*

Chapter Eight

During the following week, the first daffodils bloomed, their yellow cups a joyous change from the dreary colors that had coated the ground since the first thaw. Green leaf buds popped onto the bare, gray trees. Kate spent the week busy at home, helping her *maem* with the housework. April always meant a good spring-cleaning of the house with windows opened, furniture moved, and bedding aired outside in the morning sunshine.

She didn't mind the extra work. After all, *idle hands were the devil's breeding ground,* Maem always said. Kate also relished the reward of enjoying shiny windowpanes and dust-free corners. She didn't even mind scrubbing the bedroom floors, applying a layer of wood oil, and mopping up the excess liquid with clean rags. The chores kept her busy, which meant her mind did not wander. For that, she was most grateful.

In the afternoons, after the housework was finished and before the late milking, Maem would retreat to the bedroom, finding a few minutes to lie down before it was time to begin preparing supper. Kate used that time to return to the family garden and continue the work she loved so well, hoeing and clearing away unwanted weeds, sticks, and rocks.

Tending to the garden remained her favorite chore. She loved the feeling of the dry earth on her hands and the warm sun on the back of her neck. Becca often returned home from school and complained about working in the garden. She preferred to play with her friends who lived down the lane. Unfortunately, for Becca, they, too, needed to help at home so, with great reluctance and a lot of sighing, she would work alongside Kate for the afternoon hours. The extra hands were needed. The spring gardens needed proper care or else there would not be enough food for the families during the rest of the year.

That evening, everyone's mood seemed a little lighter than usual, all except David, who grew more despondent each day. During the supper hour, Kate watched him pick at the food on his plate, listening as her *maem* scolded him for wasting God's precious gift of food. Her words fell on deaf ears. Daed was not obviously angry, but nonetheless remained quiet, quickly retreating to the barn after the meal for final chores.

Each night, before it was time to retire, Daed called the children into the kitchen where they would kneel down for evening prayers. Most nights, David was not present, having rolled his wheelchair into his bedroom to escape the humiliation of not being able to kneel. Only then did Daed seem more himself, a little bit relaxed when his son was no longer present in the room.

It was an observation that confused Kate.

Many nights, she lay in bed, staring at the ceiling and wondering why Daed felt such anger toward David. Oh, she overheard bits and pieces of whispered discussions between Maem and Daed regarding the future of the farm and what to do with David. One option they considered was sending him to a rehabilitation center. Sometimes Kate wondered if that was merely to send him out of sight, rather than because of how much work it was to tend to the needs of a disabled, angry young man.

While Kate often felt guilt at having known of David's inclination to drink alcohol and not having informed her parents, she found herself questioning the reasons behind her parents' shame. Several times, she wanted to ask her *maem*, but she never found the courage to do so. When her *maem* was in a good, cheerful mood, Kate didn't want to ruin it. And when her *maem* seemed extra down, Kate hesitated to add to her worries. So the question remained unspoken and the answer undisclosed.

"Kate!"

She looked up from where she knelt in the garden, surprised to hear David calling her.

He sat on the porch, his wheelchair parked next to the long bench that leaned against the house. His shirt was untucked from his pants and one of his suspenders hung loose from his shoulder. Without his hat on, his hair looked tousled and bedridden. Once again, he hadn't brushed his hair.

"Come here!"

The command lacked any warmth or friendliness. With a heavy heart, she got to her feet, pausing to brush the dirt from the front of her dress before she headed toward the house. He watched her, his eyes narrowing as she neared.

"Could you walk any slower?"

She held her tongue. It would be so easy to retort his taunts. She often wished that she could. But her commitment to God was stronger than her annoyance at her brother's snide remarks and barbs. Forcing a smile on her face, she approached the porch steps.

"What is it, David?"

He gestured with his thumb toward the house. "I'm cold. Get me my blanket, will you?"

Pursing her lips, she held back a rebuke for his rudeness. No "please." No kindness. Just a command spoken with contempt. He seemed to ignore the fact that she had been working in the garden, and that with little effort, he could have most certainly fetched it himself. In typical David fashion, he preferred to inconvenience her rather than take care of himself. She wondered how long this punishing attitude would last.

Without a word, however, she walked past him and opened the kitchen door. Quietly, she padded across the floor and grabbed the crocheted blanket from the sofa. She knew her *maem* was napping, having finished the cleaning earlier and claiming a headache from so much activity. Kate knew otherwise. Her *maem*'s headaches came more frequently now that spring had arrived. Whether it was allergies or stress, Kate didn't know. Whatever it was, it would pass eventually.

Back outside, she gently laid the blanket over David's lap. "Better?"

"No."

She ignored his negative response. It was her coping mechanism for dealing with David. She had learned it from years of practice. "Want me to push your chair into the sun? It'll be warmer there."

"Why? So I can watch you garden better? I think not!"

"Suit yourself," she said, trying to sound cheerful. Each day, it was increasingly difficult to ignore the scornful remarks that he tossed in her direction. It was a game. At least that was how she saw it. The harder she tried to ignore him, the harder he tried to annoy her.

Finished with tending to David's needs, she couldn't walk away from the porch fast enough. With each step, she felt as if she could breathe a little bit easier. *Distance*, she thought. *That is the best remedy for dealing with David.* The tightness in her chest dissipated as she returned to the garden, just on the other side of the porch, and grabbed the hoe that she had set against the wire fence.

Order . . . that was what she needed in her garden, just as she needed it in her life. The rows of dirt with recently planted seeds were free of weeds and that was how she intended to keep it. She smoothed the dirt between each row, using the hoe to rake out any growing plants.

"Kate!"

She ignored him, pretending that she didn't hear him. It was easy to do. Instead of responding, she concentrated on the raking motion, counting each movement: *one, two, three.* A root emerged and she knelt down to pick it up to toss into her rubbish pile.

"Kate! I need you!"

Shutting her eyes, she clenched the muscles in her jaw. *If only the younger girls were home*, she thought as she tossed down the hoe and turned around, refusing to look in David's direction. Miriam and Becca had asked for permission to visit Susan after school, wanting to see Ruth Ann. Kate couldn't fault them for that, but she sure wished they were home now.

"Kate!" There was panic in his voice this time.

Figuring that she'd get an earful from both David and her parents for ignoring his cries of help, she picked up her pace. "I'm coming. I'm coming!" she called back.

As she rounded the corner of the house, she finally lifted her eyes to look at him. What she saw startled her. He was sprawled across the porch, his legs twisted beneath the upside-down wheelchair.

"David!" Running toward him, she instantly felt a wave of guilt. He had needed her and she had ignored him. Again. "What happened?"

"I had to wait for you, that's what happened!" He swatted at her hands as she tried to lift him. With fire in his eyes, he snapped at her. "Go get help!"

Go get help.

Immediately, Kate released David and stood up. Wasn't that what David had said the night of the accident? Only he hadn't sounded angry that night; he had sounded scared. Scared because he couldn't move. Scared because Ruth was pinned beneath him. Scared because, in the cold darkness, he sensed that everything in his life had just changed.

"I'll get Daed," she mumbled as she scrambled to her feet and ran toward the barn.

The barn was empty. She called for Daed, but he was nowhere in sight. "Daed!" she called again. No response.

The door at the back of the barn was opened. Thinking that, mayhaps, he was working out there, she ran toward it, calling his name again. But instead of finding Daed, she noticed a gray-topped buggy pulling into the driveway. Waving her arms, she ran toward the buggy, both surprised and relieved to see Samuel.

She stopped short and tried to catch her breath, one hand on the side of his buggy and the other on her chest as she gulped for air.

"What is it, Kate?"

"David. He's fallen from his chair and I can't lift him."

"Is he hurt, then?" Samuel asked as he stepped on the brake and set down the reins.

"*Nee*, I don't think so."

"Well then," Samuel said, jumping down from the buggy. "Let's go see what I can do to help, *ja*?"

He walked behind her, his long legs taking deep strides while she half ran, half walked toward the house. Clearly, her sense of urgency was not mirrored by Samuel. He remained calm and collected, the complete opposite of how Kate felt. She envied his sense of control and, as she neared the porch, realized that the only panic over the situation had come from her.

Suddenly, she felt foolish.

Samuel didn't seem to notice as he knelt beside David, resting his hand on the side of the wheelchair. "Well now," he said, drawing out each word. "Looks like you have yourself in a pickle here."

"It's not a joke," David snapped. "Get me up."

Samuel raised an eyebrow. Kate felt the color flood to her cheeks and looked away. "You can't get up by yourself, then?"

"I said get me up! I wouldn't ask if I could!"

Taking a deep breath, Samuel stood up and took his time righting the wheelchair before he reached for David's arms and lifted him into the air. Gently, he lowered David into the chair and paused to set his legs properly on the footrests. Kate leaned over to pick up the blanket and place it over his legs.

"What happened anyway?"

David scowled, his eyes darting toward Kate. "She didn't come when I called. My blanket fell and I couldn't reach it! She'd rather garden than respond when I need something!"

She noticed Samuel frown. Immediately, she saw the situation as Samuel surely did: a disabled young man in trouble and a negligent sister who didn't respond in time to help. Her shame forced her to look away, suddenly wishing that Samuel had not shown up at all. While she felt grateful for his assistance, she could do very well without him having witnessed this outburst from her brother.

"I see," Samuel said, his voice deep and thoughtful.

"Do you?" David's hands clutched at the arms of his wheelchair, his fingers curling over the edge and his knuckles white with rage. "Because if you actually do 'see,' you're the first one who actually does!"

For a moment, Samuel did not move. He seemed to digest what David said. Kate backed away from her brother, staring at the ground as she waited for Samuel to say something . . . anything to break the silence. Why hadn't she come right away when David called her? The entire situation could have been avoided and Samuel would not have been subjected to the explosive environment that was the Zook farm. But he remained silent, not responding. Instead, he merely placed his hand on David's shoulder, a gesture of comfort she noticed that took her brother by surprise.

"Best get going," he mumbled and started down the porch steps. At the bottom, he paused. Kate watched the ground, where his shadow fell on the walkway. She was startled when she saw the shadow turn back, looking over his shoulder in her direction. "Kate," he said. "You have a minute, then?"

She nodded her head, her eyes still on the ground. Without looking, she knew that David was glaring at her, his eyes boring a hole in her back.

Samuel headed down the walkway, slowing down to let Kate catch up. In silence they walked, side by side, across the driveway and through the barn. With his hands thrust into his front pockets and his head bent down, he appeared deep in thought. It gave Kate time to wonder what he thought, her fear growing that he might inquire about what David had meant.

He didn't.

On the other side of the barn, Samuel stood by his buggy. He stared at her for a long second before he tilted his head and crossed his arms over his chest. "You OK?"

His question caught her by surprise. It had been a long time since anyone inquired about how she was. She tried to think of a response, knowing that the typical answer was "*Ja.*" Only she knew he'd suspect that she was not speaking the truth. She guessed he wasn't seeking a thoughtless answer. So instead of responding, she focused on how to provide him with a good answer.

For the past four months, everything had been about David. First, the family had spent days worrying about whether he would live. Then they'd spent weeks worried about his inability to move his legs. When David had finally come home, confined to a wheelchair and the good will of others, their concern shifted to how he would adapt to all of this.

No one had ever asked how she was faring . . . whether she was OK.

No one until now.

"I . . . I . . ." She couldn't decide how to answer his question. The layers were too deep and she dared not try to peel through them. "I don't know how to answer that."

He shook his head. "Then I take it that means not well."

"I didn't mean that," she gushed, hoping that she didn't sound like she was complaining. She hadn't meant it that way. "It's just that . . . I'm not used to . . ." Flustered, she paused and tilted her head, meeting his eyes for the first time. "Why are you here anyway?"

Startled by the sudden shift of conversation, Samuel frowned. "Excuse me?"

"I mean . . . why were you here? You were pulling into the driveway when I was looking for Daed."

"Ah!" He forced a smile. "*Ja*, about that . . ."

In the distance, Kate could hear her *daed* walking in from the fields. He was talking to himself in Dutch, something she had caught him doing on more than one occasion. Her eyes flickered over Samuel's shoulders in the direction of Daed's voice. He hadn't rounded the bend yet and noticed Samuel's buggy parked next to the far end of the barn.

"I was wondering if you might be at your *aendi*'s this Saturday."

That was an unusual question, indeed! "*Ja*, I hadn't heard otherwise."

He nodded his head as if he had expected that response. "*Vell* then, I wanted to know what time you'd be walking home and," he paused as if searching for the right words. "Mayhaps you'd take a ride with me into town afterwards? We could grab a soda or something."

She almost caught her breath, realizing that he might be asking her to ride into town for a refreshment but understanding there was something grander in his invitation. Was it possible that Samuel truly wanted to get to know her better? He sure did seem to be spending a lot of time going out of his way for her.

"I . . ."

"Well hello there, Samuel!"

Samuel stood a bit straighter as he turned to greet her *daed.* "Great weather for planting."

"Clear skies and warm weather: God's way of softening the harsh blow of winter, *ja*?"

Kate took a step backward and let the two men converse, awkwardly aware that Daed had not asked why Samuel was there, as if his presence was the most natural thing in the world. Their conversation focused mostly on the crops. She almost caught herself smiling as she remembered Samuel's mother, Mary, teasingly declare that men never talked about anything besides horses, crops, and buggies.

While they stood there talking, Miriam and Becca ran down the lane, smiling and laughing as they chased each other. When they saw Samuel talking with their *daed* and Kate, they stopped running. Kate saw Becca nudge Miriam and whisper something that made her laugh. She'd deal with Becca later, she told herself.

Samuel smiled at the youngest Zook sisters. "There's a refreshing ray of sunshine or two!"

Kate blushed at the friendly greeting he bestowed on her siblings. There was something about the Esh family that seemed to make the mundane very special.

Miriam smiled and lowered her eyes. Becca, however, grinned as she glanced at Kate first and then back to Samuel.

Daed glanced at the sun overhead. "In time for chores, girls." He motioned toward the barn. "Best get started with the milking, then." His words clearly indicated that any visiting with Samuel Esh was over. Work always came before socialization.

Kate wished Daed would leave so that she could answer Samuel's question from earlier. However, she noticed with a sinking heart that Samuel took the hint from Daed and waved good-bye to everyone as he sauntered back to his buggy. With a quick look over his shoulder in Kate's direction, he smiled and winked before stepping inside and closing the door behind him.

It took her twenty minutes to clear her head. She replayed the visit in her head, analyzing everything that had just happened. First, his unexpected arrival just when she'd needed help with David. Then his reaction to the harsh criticism from her brother. Finally, his asking her to ride into town . . . on Saturday! She wondered what all of it meant and from where all of this attention originated. Samuel Esh was clearly intent on courting her. That fact could no longer be denied.

The thought both warmed her heart and chilled her blood. Why on earth was Samuel Esh so interested in her anyway?

CHAPTER NINE

For the next two days, Kate remained unusually distracted. Several times, Maem had to call her name, not just once or twice, but three times in order to get her attention. Once Daed scolded her for forgetting to milk two of the cows. And Miriam asked her if she was ill.

Kate knew that she wasn't sick. Not physically, anyway. If anything, she was sick from worry. She replayed the scene from earlier in the week when Samuel stopped by and helped her with David. The memory gave her pain: the words, the expressions, the disappointment. And, of course, there was that question about riding into town with him. She hadn't gotten the chance to answer him, since Daed had interrupted them and then the two girls returned from school.

In the afternoons, when she worked in the garden, whenever she heard a buggy in the distance, she stopped weeding, sitting back on her heels to listen. Would the buggy wheels turn into their driveway? Would Samuel visit once again? When she realized what she was doing, she scolded herself for acting so silly. Samuel had better things to do than come visit her again, especially when she hadn't answered his invitation. Surely he must have thought poorly of her for such ill manners.

And then, of course, perhaps he'd had second thoughts after reflecting on the incident with David. Mayhaps he had stopped by, intending to ask her to go riding with him, but after he'd returned home, he might have changed his mind. After all, David's embarrassing accusation that she was lazy might have chased him away.

It didn't help matters that David seemed to sense her pensiveness. As was typical when Kate was feeling down, David sought for ways to needle her even more than usual. She tried to tell herself that his bitterness was just his way of dealing with his resentment over the situation, and didn't specifically relate to her, even if she didn't always believe that.

His cutting remarks were bad when the family was around, but during this time grew increasingly malicious when no one else was around. At those times, David seemed to acquire more intensity in his efforts to disparage and belittle Kate.

On Friday, when Maem was outside in her herb garden and the house was quiet, David pushed his wheelchair close to the sofa where Kate was sewing up a tear in one of Becca's dresses.

"Don't know why you bother," he sneered. "She'll only rip it again. Climbs trees like monkeys, she does!"

While it was true, Kate merely shrugged as she threaded the needle. "I like helping Maem. One less thing for her to do."

He scoffed as he turned around the wheelchair. "*Ja vell*, I liked helping Daed before, too."

"You could still help," she said, her voice sounding meek.

"Oh really?" He glared at her, the tone of his voice changing from belittling to downright cruel. "Sure would be hard to maneuver this contraption down the line of cows for milking, don't you think?" He paused, looking in the air as if pondering something. "Oh wait, that's right. You *don't* think. That's part of the problem."

She set down her sewing, bracing herself for the verbal tornado that she sensed was ready to touch down. "David . . ."

"Don't 'David' me," he snapped, pointing a finger at her. "You have no right to 'David' me! You don't think. You've proven that time and time again. If you think I'm wrong, just go ask Jacob or Ruth." He laughed, a sinister gleam in his eyes. "What's that? You can't because they're dead?"

His obsession with Jacob and Ruth felt like a dagger in her heart each time he brought up their names. Her throat began to close in and she could barely speak. "Stop it," she managed to whisper, horrified at his heinous words.

David responded by laughing as he rolled the wheelchair away from her, apparently satisfied with the tears in Kate's eyes and sorrow in her voice. She wiped at her cheeks, ashamed for having let him see her pain. It was bad enough that she felt responsible for two deaths, and she certainly didn't need David's hateful reminders.

By the time Saturday came, she needed to get away from the house. As she walked down the road toward her *aendi*'s farm, she wondered if that was why Maem had volunteered her to help Susan. The thought kept her mind occupied as she approached the place where the wrecked buggy had loomed. It felt like the first time that she'd been able to concentrate on something besides the accident as she passed the location.

A fresh perspective on the situation presented itself. Originally, Kate presumed that Susan needed her help. Now she wondered if Maem knew how much Kate needed *to* help. If she'd set things up to provide Kate with at least one day of peace in each week.

"*Gut mariye!*" Susan greeted Kate from the porch where she hung damp clothes on the line that stretched from the roof corner to the work shed across the barnyard. White sheets, black pants, and multicolored dresses flapped in the light spring breeze. Certainly Susan had been up for hours if she was already hanging the laundry.

"Up early, then?"

Susan smiled. "Guess who began sleeping through the night!"

Kate smiled. "Really?"

Susan nodded, reaching down for a towel to hang from the line. "*Ja*, really! She skipped her two o'clock feeding! Why, I feel fit as a fiddle today!"

"Sleep will do that for you."

Grabbing the last towel from the basket, Susan pinned it to the line and then pushed the clothes farther out by moving the pulley. "All right! Now that is done and I have time to visit before I go help Timothy!" She turned to Kate and put her hands on her hips. "How about a nice cup of coffee and a chat? The Lord doesn't mind a little break from chores once in a while."

The coffee percolated on the stove as Kate waited for Susan to join her at the table. She missed the days when Susan lived with her family. Her bubbly personality, so contrary to Maem's, always seemed to brighten any day. In many ways, and in spite of their differences, Becca and Susan's personalities favored each other while Miriam and Kate's took after Maem.

"Haven't been to your house in a while," Susan said as she poured the coffee into two mugs. "How are things going, anyway?"

Kate shrugged, not wanting to say anything negative for fear of being perceived as complaining.

Susan saw through it. "Not better then, I take it?"

"I didn't say that."

Susan laughed. "You didn't have to. I have eyes, Kate. I can see for myself how things have changed." She blew on her coffee before taking a sip. "Plus Becca told me, too."

Ah, so there it was. The truth. During their visit, Miriam and Becca must have confided in their *aendi*. Kate could guess that Becca had made a comment that caused Susan to question them further. Kate could only imagine what they would have told Susan, certainly enough to let her know that a dark cloud hung over the Zooks' household.

"It's to be expected, I guess," Kate mumbled. "I mean . . . everything is different now. There's so much uncertainty. This is a change." She looked up. "A big change for all of us."

"Big change, eh?" From the expression on Susan's face, Kate could tell that she was not convinced.

"For Daed and Maem, especially."

Susan frowned. "How so?"

Kate didn't feel like talking about it. She'd rehashed the details so many times in her own head. Saying them out loud made the reality that much harsher. She looked forward to coming to Susan's house in order to escape the dark reality of what had happened and the toll it had taken on her family. "Their lives have changed forever, I reckon. Who will take over the farm? David can't do it now, and Thomas has his own family and farm."

"I reckon that's true," Susan admitted.

"And when they get old, they have to worry about David's care as well as their own. And then, when they are no longer with us, who will take care of David? That must weigh heavily on their minds, don't you think?"

"*Ja*, I do."

"Ain't no more boys," Kate added, as if she truly needed to point that out. "I'm doing what I can to make up for it."

Susan set down her coffee mug and stared at Kate. For a long moment, she remained silent, as if mulling over what Kate said. The clock ticked in the silence, the gentle rhythm of the pendulum soothing Kate's frayed nerves.

"Do you think it's your responsibility to make up for it, Kate? Do you think you really can?" Susan shook her head. "*Nee*, Kate. This is not your cross to bear."

Then why does it feel as though it's my responsibility? The question almost burst from her lips. She wanted to ask. And she knew that talking to Susan would release the burden from her shoulders. But she couldn't. Susan didn't know the truth. Susan didn't know that Kate could have prevented the accident. If Kate had ridden home that night with David and Ruth, if she had taken the reins, insisting that he not drive the buggy, if she had alerted Ruth or anyone else that David was intoxicated . . . but no. The fact that she, and she alone, could have prevented his injury and Ruth's death was something Susan probably couldn't imagine.

"Mayhaps not," Kate said, more out of politeness than because she agreed with Susan. "It's not quite five months yet. Reckon we all just need more time."

From the bedroom at the top of the stairs, Ruth Ann began to cry. Susan glanced in the direction of the noise and sighed. "Well, more time is not something we have right now."

Susan started to stand up, but Kate stopped her. "I'll get the *boppli*," she said, grateful that the conversation had been interrupted. Truth be told, Kate felt uncomfortable airing the situation at home to anyone, even Susan. She'd made a mental reminder to talk with Miriam about curtailing Becca's loose tongue in the future. Their youngest sister's bad habit of talking without thinking would come back to haunt all of them one day.

Upstairs, Kate entered the baby's room. It was dark, with drawn shades blocking the light. Kate moved to the window and lifted the shade, bright sunlight flooding the room. Small specks of dust floated in the sunbeams and Kate made a mental note to thoroughly clean the room later that morning. A simple room with just a crib, changing table, and rocking chair, it was typical of most Amish nurseries, although many parents simply let the newborns sleep in their own bedroom.

She cooed at the *boppli*, who stopped crying when she appeared. She glanced at the dresses hung from small hangers, miniature versions of an Amish woman's dress, and selected the green one. Kate set it on the changing table and hurried over to pick up the *boppli*. She nuzzled Ruth Ann's neck, breathing in the sweet scent of talcum powder, as she carried the baby over to the changing table. Within minutes, she had Ruth Ann dressed and the crib tidied. With the baby on her hip, Kate carried her downstairs, all the while talking softly in Dutch to her.

The day seemed to fly by. She never felt as if she was actually working when she spent the day tending to Ruth Ann. During Ruth Ann's late morning nap, she managed to clean the kitchen and fold the dry clothes from the line. Then, after feeding Ruth Ann at noon, she took her for a nice walk, the hand-me-down stroller fighting the gravel of the lane toward the back fields.

By the time four o'clock rolled around, supper was ready, the kitchen smelled of cooked ham and fresh rolls, and Ruth Ann was napping on a blanket that Kate had placed on the floor in a sunbeam in the sitting room.

She wasn't in a hurry to get home. She knew that Miriam and Becca would be helping Daed with the late milking. Still, she was eager to see if Maem needed any help with David. It would have been a long day for her, tending to his needs while the other two girls helped Daed. With tomorrow being a worship day, everyone would bathe that evening starting with David who, as usual, would fight off help every step of the way. Maem liked to have him bathed first so that by the time Daed came in, David was already in his bedroom.

After saying good-bye to her *aendi* and kissing the *boppli*'s soft head, she started walking home. Her mind was fixed on the conversation that she'd shared with Susan earlier. If only Susan knew what it was really like, living with the constant reminder of the ramifications from that night: Dad's anger, Maem's headaches, David's bitterness.

A buggy rolled down the hill, approaching her from the opposite direction. She didn't think much of it until she noticed the horse slow down as it neared. When it was close enough, the horse stopped and a familiar face looked out the open door, smiling in greeting.

"Good afternoon, Kate Zook!"

She lifted her hand and waved. Samuel Esh surely had a way of surprising her.

"Why don't you jump in? I'll give you a ride home."

"It's just a short walk if I cut through the Yoders' fields," she said, gesturing up the road. "Plus, you look to be headed the other way." While she certainly noticed and appreciated his kindness over the past few weeks, she didn't want to inconvenience him. Surely he was headed home after running errands.

He didn't look deterred. "I can turn the buggy around easy enough, I reckon."

When he tilted back his straw hat and lifted his eyebrows at her, she relented and smiled. "All right, then."

Once again, he waited until she was situated before slapping the reins on the horse's back and clucking his tongue to urge the horse forward. He continued down the road, not saying anything as he looked for a place where he could turn around. She listened to the gentle whirling noise of the buggy wheels against the road and found herself lost, just for a moment, in the peacefulness of sitting next to Samuel in his buggy.

She took a deep breath and relaxed. She sensed his eyes on her, but he remained silent. She wished that she could think of something to say, something beyond just commenting on the weather or inquiring about what errands he had run that day. Her timid nature in conversing with men kept her tongue-tied.

To her surprise, he did not turn into the lane beyond Susan's house to turn around. Instead, he continued driving the buggy.

"You missed the turnaround," she pointed out.

"*Ja*, I sure did."

"You didn't have to take the long route," she said. "It's . . . it's not as painful passing it anymore. Someone moved the buggy."

"Did they now?" The mischievous smile on his lips told her that he kept a secret.

For a brief moment, she wondered if he had anything to do with its disappearance, a question that she did not feel comfortable asking. However, her curiosity was definitely piqued by his cheerful look and the sparkle in his blue eyes. Once again, she found his temperament contagious, a refreshing breath of fresh air after so many months of solemnity in her family's house.

Trying to appear serious, he looked at her. "Sure does feel a little warm out, don't you think?"

The sun shone in the sky and the clouds floated peacefully over the horizon. But the air was still cool, even though April had arrived. "Not particularly."

He tugged at the collar of his white shirt. "I was thinking about stopping in town for some ice cream. You don't mind now, do you?"

"Ice cream?" She tried not to laugh. "In April?"

He grinned, "You never did answer me when I stopped by this week to ask about going into town. I reckon I'm just presuming that your silence could just as likely mean yes as it could mean no."

His flawless logic made her laugh. "That is one way to look at it."

"Besides, you look like a girl . . . a young woman," he corrected himself, "that could use a spin into town and a nice ice cream. While I'm not a betting kind of man, I reckon I'm not too far off the mark that you, Kate Zook, are someone who deserves some nice things from time to time. So," he said, turning to stare at her.

"What do you say, Kate? Would you ride into town with me for that ice cream?"

Kate suddenly understood what he meant by his question. Her cheeks colored and she looked out the window for a moment, a smile on her lips even though she tried to hide it. She had suspected his intentions when he insisted on walking her home from the singing. She further grasped his purpose after he'd taken her on the fishing excursion, asking her *daed* and not her directly. Now, he was informally asking her a question that, depending on her answer, could change her future.

"Well?"

She bit her lower lip, listening to the words in her head that conflicted with the pounding of her heart. For too long, she seemed to follow her common sense and not her instinct. This time, she told herself, she would do no such thing.

Lifting her head, she stared at him, letting her eyes meet his as she said, "I think ice cream sounds like a *wunderbar gut* idea, Samuel Esh."

He smiled, nodding his head once in acknowledgment of what was said without words. They rode the rest of the way into town in silence, a calm sense of serenity in the buggy.

Chapter Ten

She caught him staring at her while the bishop preached. Daniel and Jane King, the family holding the worship service that week, sat in the front row next to the other preachers and their wives, the men facing the women. She'd looked up because she suddenly felt the sensation that she was being watched. It only took a few seconds to notice Samuel staring directly at her. He was sitting amid the other young unmarried men and smiled, just slightly, when their eyes met.

She blushed and looked away.

Verna sat on one side of her while Hannah sat on the other. Both young women sat still as statues, having been taught from a young age to never fidget in church. Kate, however, found it hard to sit still and listen to the bishop. His voice droned on and on, and the warmth of the room made her feel sleepy. However, once she realized that she was under scrutiny, any drowsiness she felt disappeared.

The previous day's trip to town for ice cream hadn't taken longer than an hour. For most of the way there, they hadn't spoken. After Samuel paid the cashier, they'd sat on a bench outside of the ice cream parlor. It seemed easier to talk to him when they were not confined to the buggy. Slowly, she began to feel more at ease in his presence and felt comfortable enough to smile when he teasingly pointed out that ice cream had dripped onto her chin.

"Oh bother!" She wiped at it with the back of her hand.

He laughed at her. "That didn't make it any better. Here, let me do it." Without waiting for permission, he brushed his finger across her chin, his gentle touch sending a wave of tingles down her spine. "There! Now you are ice cream free."

On the ride home, conversation flowed even more easily. Samuel did most of the talking, telling her stories about his travels across the country during his *rumschpringe*. She listened intently, occasionally asking him questions, especially when he talked about New York City.

"Those buildings are so tall, Kate! Why, you can scarce find a tree anywhere, except in Central Park!"

"I can't imagine it!" she had replied. "No trees? Who would ever want to live like that?"

Samuel shook his head. "And when I went to Los Angeles, it was even worse. Just roads and cars and buildings. Concrete everywhere!"

"Oh my!"

He nodded. "But don't get me wrong, Kate. There were beautiful places along the way. We stopped to camp in the Grand Canyon. That was a sight you just cannot describe. The power of God's creation is truly stunning. It's important to appreciate it." He paused, as if a thought struck him. "I reckon even the cities have beauty in them. I liked some of the architecture."

She frowned and tilted her head, unfamiliar with the word he was using.

"The building design." He smiled as he explained. "Some of the buildings are simply breathtaking . . . a true testament to man's ability to create something from God's materials, the simple things that He created on earth, and transform it into something even more beautiful."

"Even if there are no trees?"

He laughed. "Even if there are no trees."

Kate shook her head. "Well, that's not for me." She licked her ice cream cone. "I'm perfectly happy here. I don't need to go see big buildings or concrete playgrounds, although I do confess I imagine the Grand Canyon is breathtaking."

"So no wild *rumschpringe*, Kate Zook?"

She laughed at his gentle teasing. "*Nee*, Samuel."

"Just an ice cream on a Saturday afternoon?"

She tried to hide her smile, knowing full well that her cheeks turned pink. "That'll have to do, I reckon," she managed to say.

"Can't say I'm unhappy knowing that, Kate," he had replied. "If this is as wild as you get, you sure do seem to have your priorities straight."

Now, sitting on the hard bench at worship service, she turned those words over in her mind once again. Did he really feel that way about her? That she had her priorities straight? The night before, she'd tossed and turned, worried that when he found out the truth, he would be disappointed. He would learn that nothing could be further from the truth. Certainly, her priorities had not been straight back in December. And it wasn't the first time. Would he think she was deceptive?

She looked down at her hands in her lap, fighting the urge to once again raise her head and meet his gaze. She wondered about his *rumschpringe*. Why had he felt compelled to travel and see the world? What had made him unhappy in Lancaster County? Had he been seeking something out in the world of the Englische only to find that they had nothing to offer?

When he'd left on his *rumschpringe*, tongues wagged about that Esh boy, leaving his family farm and only sending postcards home as a way of communicating. Yet his parents hadn't seemed to mind his desire to travel; they even expressed confidence that he would return home. And when he did, he returned a man. That was almost three years ago now.

From what Kate knew, for the first two years back, he'd focused on the farm and his friends. And then he began courting Ella. Kate hadn't given much thought about Samuel Esh, really. She'd figured he was destined to marry Ella. After all, courtship was not about casually dating, but about moving toward that holy union.

Personally, she couldn't imagine leaving home to travel so far away. She thought she recalled that Samuel traveled with a cousin from Ohio, but she wasn't exactly certain. Samuel hadn't mentioned his travel companions by name, just using the generic "we." Still, Kate figured that it must have been lonely, away from family and friends.

She felt Verna nudge her.

"Kneel, silly," she whispered to Kate.

Quickly, Kate slid off the bench and turned around, kneeling with her face in her hands. She prayed for the strength to accept her weaknesses and sins. She prayed that she might make better decisions as she strove to honor the Ordnung. And she prayed for David and her parents, wishing that God's will might help them deal with his disability in a more positive way.

"What were you thinking about during service, Kate?"

She was helping to set the table when Verna asked her that question. Jane Yoder had directed the younger women to tend to that job while the other older women began dishing out the plates of food. Shrugging her shoulders, Kate didn't answer.

"Could it be that you're a bit *ferhoodled*?"

"Verna!" But the color rose to Kate's cheeks, giving away her answer.

"I wondered that." Verna leaned closer and whispered. "I'm glad."

Courtship was a private matter, not something that people tended to openly share. It was better that way, just in case the couple decided to part company. No questions needed to be asked or answered. However, Samuel certainly didn't seem to be hiding his interest in Kate. Now she knew that others had noticed that, too.

She wondered what others thought, and wished that she could ask Verna. But Kate didn't want to be seen as acting proud, and since Ella seemed to have lingering feelings toward him, it didn't seem right to bring it up.

After the first seating, Kate quickly helped to clear the plates and reset the table. As always, it was simple fare for the Sunday dinner: sliced bread, applesauce, cold cuts, cup cheese, pretzels, and pickles. Miriam and Becca had eaten already and left with Daed to return home.

"Sure was fun fishing last week."

It took a moment for Kate to realize that Sylvia was speaking to her. Kate had shied away from socializing for such a long time that it didn't come naturally. Usually she avoided sitting with the younger women or ate quickly so that she could help with the cleanup.

She smiled and tried to come up with a polite reply. "*Ja*, and the weather has been holding up nicely, too. Daffodils and forsythia are blooming right nice," she said.

"We're going to go to the park this afternoon to walk a spell. You want to join us, then?"

Kate sighed. Daed would need her help, and Maem would surely need a break from David. "*Danke*, but I best say no."

"Well, we'll see you tonight at the singing, *ja*?"

Kate wondered the same question. Daed hadn't said anything about taking her, and she didn't feel comfortable asking. "Mayhaps," she responded. More than likely, she'd stay at home. There was a lot of work to do in the morning.

She slipped away after eating. The walk home would only take about fifteen minutes, but she was eager to escape the gathering. She wanted to go home, get changed, and see what she could do to help her *maem* before evening chores.

"Hey, Kate!"

She stopped walking and turned around, surprised to see Samuel jogging to catch up with her.

"Mind if I walk you home?"

She smiled, glancing over his shoulder to see a buggy approaching. "It's a nice day for walking, *ja?*"

He fell into step beside her, his hands in his pockets and his hat tilted backward on his head. "That it is. And Easter is next week. Pretty soon it will be summer, I reckon."

The buggy passed them, the driver an older Amish man with a long white beard. He lifted his hand and waved in greeting. Both Kate and Samuel returned the gesture. As the buggy continued down the road, Kate noticed three little faces staring out the back window, watching them as they walked.

"Going anywhere this summer, Kate?"

She glanced at him and laughed. "*Nee!* Who has time to go anywhere?"

His lifted his shoulders and shrugged. "My cousin is taking his family to Ohio to visit his *fraa*'s family. I was thinking about tagging along."

Wanderlust, she thought. Hadn't he gotten that out of his system during his *rumschpringe*? "That would be nice."

"Maybe in July. Not as much work on the farm then."

She wished that she could say the same. But Samuel had brothers to help his *daed*. And the Esh family didn't have a David in their life.

"And I heard that there's a youth trip being planned to go to Appalachia to help build some houses for the needy," he continued. "Ever think about doing that, Kate?"

She shook her head. "I . . . I can't leave David," she heard herself say.

"Oh," he replied solemnly. "I see."

Do you? David's words from the other day popped into her head. Kate cringed at the memory of the horrible things that David had said in front of Samuel. It made her wonder even more at Samuel's continued interest in her.

"Well then, we can plan day trips, Kate!" He turned around and walked backward, facing her as he did so. "A picnic, perhaps?"

She caught herself laughing at his enthusiasm. It felt good to laugh, and for the briefest of moments she forgot about David.

"And a campfire with my *bruder* John and Esther. We can sing a spell and cook marshmallows!" He looked delighted with his ideas, which made her laugh even more. "We'll do a summer of adventures so that you have fun, Kate. I think you haven't had a lot of fun recently. You need more of it."

She wanted to ask him why. Why was this important to him? Why did he care? Instead, she lowered her eyes and took a deep breath. "A picnic would be nice, Samuel."

They approached the mailbox at the end of her parents' driveway. Samuel continued walking with her toward the house. She had thought he would turn around to go back to the Kings' house to fetch his buggy. Instead, he appeared comfortable walking up to hers.

"Reckon I might visit a spell with David," he said. "Seems he could use some cheering up."

Kate didn't know if that was possible but didn't say so. Cheering up David was something no one had successfully attempted in the past five months. Still, she wasn't about to deny either Samuel or

David the chance. There was something contagious about Samuel's zest for life. Mayhaps some time together would help David after all.

There was a flurry of activity in the kitchen when they entered. David sat at the window, staring outside while Miriam and Becca played Scrabble at the table. Kate could tell that Miriam was winning because Becca was standing up, a feverish scowl on her face as she scrutinized the game board.

"Not fair! You know more words than me!"

Miriam pursed her lips and shook her head. "You say that every time you lose."

"Well, it's true!"

"Girls!" Maem hurried out of David's bedroom, carrying a book in her hands, which she handed to him. "Becca, if you can't play nicely, don't play at all!"

Just as Becca was about to respond, she caught sight of Kate and Samuel standing in the doorway. Her mouth dropped open, and then she grinned. With great exaggeration, she leaned over and nudged Miriam, gesturing in the direction of the door.

"David," Kate called out. "Samuel's come to visit you."

He barely turned his head to greet the visitor. "Why?"

"David!" she gasped, horrified at his tone. How could he speak in such a manner when Samuel had made the effort to come visiting?

Samuel laid his hand on Kate's arm and smiled. "It's OK, Kate."

Kate lowered her eyes, ashamed for her brother. In many ways, she had developed an immunity to his acrimonious words and comments. However, hearing him direct his hostility toward Samuel made her realize how ugly his tone of voice sounded. After all, it was one thing to talk to the family that way. But to Samuel?

Samuel seemed nonplussed. Instead of recoiling at the cutting remark from David, he merely ignored it. Crossing the room, he paused to greet Miriam and Becca, then smiled at Kate's *maem* before he sat next to David at the window. "You missed a right *gut* sermon today, David," Samuel began, lowering his voice as he spoke.

Kate moved across the kitchen, paying no attention to Becca's grin, and stood nearby to listen to the conversation between Samuel and her brother. Her heart beat fast as she watched him. With his curly brown hair and tanned skin, he looked handsome sitting on the rocking chair, leaning forward as he talked to David.

"Bishop preached about the resurrection and Jesus's sacrifice. He spoke a lot about personal sacrifice. I found it quite compelling."

Kate had to think back to the sermon. How had she not heard it? Then she remembered that she had been distracted, thinking about Samuel as he watched her. Yet, he had heard every word the bishop said while she'd let her mind wander. Just another sin she'd have to pray for God to forgive.

"Mayhaps you might like to attend church next service," Samuel offered. "I know my cousin would be glad to see you."

David frowned. "No point in going."

"Well, I beg to differ," Samuel retorted, leaning back in the rocking chair. "You might find a lot of comfort in being back with the young men and socializing."

Maem motioned to Kate that she was going upstairs. When she pointed to her head, Kate knew that she had another headache. Without being asked, she poured a glass of water and opened the cabinet for pain reliever. She didn't want to leave the kitchen, didn't want to miss hearing Samuel's voice as he talked with David. But she knew Maem would appreciate the medicine, so she went upstairs with it.

"*Danke*, Kate," Maem said as she took the glass. "Such a thoughtful girl."

Kate hurried to the window and pulled down the shade. "You should get those headaches checked out, Maem. They seem to be getting worse."

In reality, Kate recognized a pattern developing. Whenever left alone with David for extended periods of time, Maem needed a few hours of quiet time to recuperate. She wondered if David had noticed. *Probably*, she thought. He noticed everything about everyone else.

"When Samuel leaves, you should go help your Daed with chores."

"I will."

"And Miriam can prepare the evening supper. I have everything ready. She just needs to warm it up." She sank into her bed and sighed. "You can tell her that, *ja*?"

Kate nodded. "Of course, Maem. You just relax a spell."

Back downstairs, Kate was disappointed to see that Samuel was no longer in the kitchen. She worried that David had said something horrible, something that sent Samuel away. Miriam and Becca were focused on their game.

"Did he leave, then?" She had only been gone for a few minutes. Why had he left so suddenly?

"Your beau?" Becca asked, her eyes on the game. "He said he'd be right back."

"And don't call him that," Kate whispered in case Samuel reappeared unexpectedly. She sat down beside Miriam and glanced at her tiles.

"Hey! No helping her! That's not fair!"

"Life isn't fair." David pushed away from the window and rolled over to the table. He looked at the board for a long minute before reaching out and swiping at it with his hand. Tiles flew through the air and Becca jumped up from her seat.

"What'd you do that for?"

"Why do you care? You were losing anyway!"

Kate scrambled to her feet and began picking up the tiles. Heaven forbid Samuel walked in to see what David had just done.

"Stop picking those up, Kate."

She paused and looked up, surprised to see Samuel standing at the doorway. His expression was changed. Gone was the jovial smile and sparkling eyes. In its place was a scowl, as if a cloud of darkness shadowed his face.

Without question, she got back to her feet.

"David, you pick up those tiles," Samuel said.

David laughed. "Are you serious? I can't pick them up."

"You had no right to ruin the girls' game. And Kate should not clean up after you." He walked toward her, reaching out to touch her arm and gently pull her away from the mess. "You did it. You clean it."

Becca watched with wide eyes and Miriam looked down at her hands in her lap. Kate, however, could only stare at Samuel, speechless at the transformation in him. "I . . . I don't mind," she whispered.

"I do."

David pushed his wheelchair away from the table and crossed his arms over his chest, defiantly glaring at Samuel.

Samuel placed his hand on Miriam's shoulder. "Girls, let's go outside and leave David to figure out how to fix this wrong. He might not be able to walk, but he sure can still use his brain."

No one questioned him. Miriam quietly stood up, pausing to set down three tiles that had landed in her lap. Becca practically ran to the door while Samuel guided Miriam and Kate outside and onto the porch. They could hear David grumbling from inside the kitchen and the sound of a kitchen chair falling over.

Kate turned to look at Samuel. "We really shouldn't leave him alone."

"I beg to differ," he replied. "What he needs is more alone time, Kate. Time to think about behaving better and trying harder. The sacrifice was done months ago. It shouldn't still be happening."

He directed them down the porch steps. "Let's take a nice walk, shall we? See how many robins we can see."

Becca and Miriam ran off ahead of them, turning down the dirt lane that ran through the farm and toward the back fields. Kate walked beside him, her mind reeling over what had just happened. Had Samuel witnessed David's outburst? Had he truly just spoken so harshly to David? She worried that David would call out for Maem, disturbing her sleep. Or what if he fell again and couldn't get up? For a moment, she almost turned around to hurry back to the house.

"Don't even think about it," he said, as if reading her mind. "It's a beautiful day and you deserve some fresh air, Kate."

She wasn't so certain about that, but said nothing in response.

"The way I look at it," he began. "David is unhappy and seems intent on making others unhappy, too. That's sure not the way to live, Kate. You are entitled to walks and smiles and laughter." He paused. "And respect."

Her feet stopped moving. "Respect?"

Samuel stood before her. "*Ja*, Kate. When he behaves so poorly and expects you to clean up after him, he is disrespecting you." He glanced up at the sky as two birds flew overhead. "The way I see it is no one should be disrespectful to my girl."

She caught her breath. Had she heard him correctly?

He reached down and touched her hand, his fingers entwining with hers. Gently, he squeezed her hand and lifted it toward his lips. After softly kissing the back of her hand, he smiled. The sparkle was back in his eyes. "Unless you feel otherwise, of course."

She didn't know how to respond. Just a few short weeks ago, his attention had seemed to come out of nowhere. Now he was professing his affection and, with that, his intentions for a possible future together. She knew these things happened. She just never thought they would happen to her.

"I . . ." She paused, uncertain how to respond. "*Nee*, Samuel," she finally said, lifting her eyes to meet his. "I don't feel otherwise."

One more kiss on her hand, and then he released it. "Good!" he announced with flourish. Gone was the solemn Samuel from inside the house. He grinned as he started walking again. "Now that we have that settled, let's see how many robins we can count. Can't let Becca win too easily, now, can we?"

Thirty minutes and twelve robins later, they returned to the house. The kitchen was quiet and, to Kate's amazement, the Scrabble tiles were picked up. For a moment, she worried that Maem cleaned them until she noticed the broom and long-handled dustpan in the corner. *Clever*, she thought, impressed that Samuel had influenced David to actually take responsibility for cleaning up his own mess for once.

"I reckon I best get going," Samuel said. "Time for chores soon." He started to walk toward the door but hesitated. "I reckon you won't mind if I swing by here to pick you up for the singing tonight, then?"

Too aware that Becca and Miriam heard him, she flushed and looked down at the floor. "I hadn't asked my *daed* about going."

Samuel tried to hide his smile. "No worries there. I already asked him."

Kate's mouth dropped. So that was where he'd gone when she'd been upstairs with Maem! He must have gone out to the barn to speak to her *daed*. She couldn't even imagine how *that* conversation went. Yet, part of her was glad that Samuel had thought to be so polite. Acknowledging an intention to court someone's daughter was unusual but not unheard of among the Amish. For Kate, knowing that Samuel had already spoken to her *daed*, and apparently received his blessing, lifted a burden of uncertainty from her shoulders.

"I'll take your silence for a yes again, and I'll be here by six." He gave her a friendly wink before disappearing through the door. She stood in the middle of the kitchen, staring after him. In such a short period of time, so much seemed to have changed. Was it possible that the dark cloud hanging over their house was slowly lifting?

Chapter Eleven

Later that evening, Kate was at the sink with Miriam, washing and drying the supper plates when she heard the sound of horse's hooves clattering on the driveway. Miriam glanced up and looked out the window, gasping when she saw the buggy.

"What is it?" Kate asked and peered over Miriam's shoulder. "Oh help!"

Samuel stopped the open-topped buggy at the corner of the barn and got out to tie up the horse before heading to the house. She hadn't expected him to arrive for her in a courting buggy. And she never would have imagined Samuel Esh owning one that looked like this one!

Unlike most courting buggies, which were handed down from brother to brother or shared with cousins, this one appeared to be brand-new. And it was varnished wood instead of painted black. The front seat was padded and covered in a deep-royal-blue velour. From the looks of it, this was one of the first times Samuel had driven it. There wasn't one speck of dust or dirt on the metal wheels.

Kate turned around and covered her face with her hands. "That's so . . ."

"So what?" Becca asked as she ran over to the window, standing on her tippy-toes to peer out the window. When she saw the buggy, she began to giggle.

"So open!" In an open buggy, everyone would see them arrive. It was a public acknowledgment of their courtship, and one that Kate wasn't certain she felt prepared to make. So far as she knew, Samuel never had driven in the courting buggy with Ella.

Becca made a face at Kate. "I thought he wasn't your beau!"

"Hush yourself!" Miriam hissed, chasing her with a damp dish-cloth. "Leave her be!"

Becca skipped away, laughing as she called out. "Maem! Best be planting more celery in the garden! Bet we'll be having a wedding this fall! Samuel's come calling for Kate in a courting buggy!"

"Becca!" Miriam and Kate said it in unison, but Becca ignored them, running up the stairs to share the good news with her *maem*.

Since the door was open, Kate could only pray that Samuel hadn't heard her sister. But when she let him inside, the playful smirk on his face told Kate that her prayer was too late.

"What's this I hear about the Zooks starting a celery farm?" he teased, removing his hat as he stepped inside.

Kate stared at the floor, her cheeks turning bright pink. "I'm so sorry," she whispered, wishing that she could throttle Becca for having shouted that.

He laughed. "Whatever for, Kate? Personally, I happen to be quite fond of celery."

Lifting her eyes, she managed to smile at him. He always seemed to say the right thing. His relaxed mannerism and play-ful teasing had a magical way of disarming her. She immediately calmed down as she realized that he hadn't taken offense at Becca's words, especially her teasing about planting extra celery, an unspo-ken indication among the Amish that a wedding was expected in the upcoming months.

During the ride to the youth singing at the Kings' house, Samuel talked about his upcoming week and the spring recital at the schoolhouse on Wednesday afternoon. "You planning on going to it?" he asked.

She shook her head. "*Nee.* Maem will want to go, so I should stay with David, I reckon." She noticed the muscles in his jaws tense at the mention of her brother. "Can't leave him alone for too long."

He stared straight ahead and did not respond.

His silence startled her. Had she said something to upset him? Rather than ask, she remained silent, rethinking what she had said and worrying about why he seemed disturbed. The encounter with David earlier certainly had not set well with Samuel. However, she sensed that something else was afoot. She knew he'd tell her if he wanted to. It wasn't her place to pry into his business.

When they reached their destination, Kate saw that several of the young men who'd arrived early were outside playing volleyball. Samuel waved to them, glancing briefly at Kate and smiling when he saw her chew on her lower lip.

"You like playing volleyball?" he asked as he directed the horse to pull up alongside the last buggy. The tension from the moment before was gone; the pensive, quiet Samuel replaced by the one with sparkling eyes and a teasing tone.

"Haven't played it in a while." Truth was that she felt uncomfortable playing sports. Even when she had attended school, she preferred reading to running around the school yard.

"So I take that answer to mean yes," he said, laughing. She groaned but couldn't hide her smile as she did. Once again, her reluctance to answer right away had put her in the position of agreeing.

"I reckon I could give it a try," she said. "Just don't hold out much hope for our side, Samuel."

He laughed again as he stepped on the brake and dropped the reins. "No disappointments, I promise," he teased and reached for her hand, holding it a few seconds longer than necessary as he helped her down from the buggy.

It turned out the volleyball teams were short more than a few players, so Samuel and Kate found themselves warmly welcomed. Despite her feelings toward sports, Kate joined the side that most needed teammates, greeting those around her with a shy smile. She knew they had witnessed her arrival with Samuel and certainly speculated about their courtship. If she had wanted to hide it, that was impossible now.

"Kate! Get it!" someone yelled from the row of players behind her.

To her surprise, she managed to hit the volleyball back over the net. When it bounced off the ground, a friendly cheer erupted from her teammates and Samuel gently clapped her on the back.

"Well done, Kate!"

She smiled, pleased with his compliment and not quite certain how to respond. Not wanting to look proud, she felt that she had to say something. "Just luck, I'm sure," she finally responded.

"If that's luck, let's keep it going!" John called out.

They were still playing when Kate noticed a buggy pull in, pausing just briefly before parking next to Samuel's. When two young women emerged, she almost caught her breath: one of them was Ella. With her dark-green dress and crisply starched prayer *kapp*, she was the image of a perfect Amish woman. Kate glanced at Samuel, wondering if he had noticed her arrival at the gathering, but it looked like either he hadn't noticed or was choosing not to pay attention.

Kate tried to return her attention to the game but couldn't help noticing the way Ella's eyes were drawn to Samuel, a look of anguish on her face. Seeing the jilted woman's reaction told Kate more than she cared to know. Clearly Ella still held feelings for Samuel.

"Watch out, Kate!"

Just in time, she turned as the volleyball missed her shoulder. She smiled apologetically and gestured toward Verna. "Mind if I step out? I'm getting tired," she said.

Verna and Hannah sat on two folding chairs on a patch of grass near the refreshment table. When they saw Kate headed in their direction, Verna quickly retrieved a third chair and set it next to Hannah's.

"My, my," Verna said. "I saw that great volley, Kate! I never knew you had it in you."

Hannah laughed at Verna's teasing. "Think about how many games we could have won back at school when we played against the boys!"

Kate sat down and shook her head. "Trust me: that was just luck."

A group of women approached the refreshment table, Ella among them. Kate fidgeted in her chair and smoothed down her skirt. While Kate liked to think that she was on friendly terms with all of the young women in the *g'may*, her tendency toward shyness meant that her close friends were limited in number. Ella was older and seemed to be on friendlier terms with Esther and Sylvia as well as a few of the other unmarried women further into their twenties. Her reputation as a righteous woman was well known among the community.

Kate's awareness of Ella's presence made her feel uncomfortable. She couldn't help but wonder what had happened between Samuel and Ella. It was impossible to think of either one doing something distasteful, something that might cause one to quit the other. That thought worried Kate more than anything else, forcing her to remain perplexed over Samuel's interest in her. Even more troublesome was her increasing anxiety that whatever had occurred between Samuel and Ella might not truly be over and, one day, he might want to return to his previous girlfriend.

"Did you hear me, Kate?"

She snapped out of her thoughts and returned her attention to Verna. "I'm sorry, what did you say?"

Hannah removed her eyeglasses and wiped them on the edge of her black apron. "*Ferhoodled*," she mumbled.

"Hannah!" Kate glanced over her shoulder, hoping that no one else overheard.

"Everyone saw that fancy courting buggy of Samuel's," Verna said, her voice low enough so that Kate didn't have to worry about eavesdroppers. "Heard he bought it just the other week from Pequea."

"I wish you wouldn't talk about it." Kate felt the heat rise to the tips of her ears.

Slipping her glasses back on, Hannah raised her eyebrow. "I heard his *maem* was right put out by how much he spent on it."

"I can only imagine!" Verna leaned forward. "But I also heard he worked an extra job for four months or so to pay for it!"

At this news, Kate perked up. An extra job? Certainly he had planned the purchase of that courting buggy long ago and that obviously meant he had intended to buy it for courting Ella that spring. Now, however, it was Kate riding beside him, not Ella.

"Doing what, Verna?" Kate asked.

She shrugged her shoulders. "Don't quote me on this, but I heard he worked evenings at the Smart Shopper. Stocking shelves or something like that."

"You'd think he'd want to save his money up for something more important than a courting buggy, at least that's what I say."

Kate glanced at Hannah, surprised by the comment. The courting buggy did seem like a frivolous purchase, especially when, most likely, he had access to other buggies. With so many children in the family and Samuel being one of the older unmarried sons, he would need to save his money for purchasing a farm for his future family. Certainly the Esh farm would pass down to one of Samuel's younger brothers. Samuel's parents were not old enough yet to retire to the *grossdaadihaus* and, with younger children still in the house, they wouldn't be for quite a few years. By that time, Samuel would be well situated on his own farm, wherever and whenever he managed to buy it. However, to Hannah's point, spending thousands of dollars on a new courting buggy was money not saved for that future farm.

Frivolous. It wasn't a word that she would have associated with Samuel. Turning around, her eyes searched the crowd of young men until she spotted him. He was laughing with Isaac and another young man. The volleyball game was winding down, and the young men were talking and laughing as they headed back toward the barn where the singing would take place.

As he walked past where Kate sat with her friends, he caught her eye and smiled. There was nothing irresponsible or thoughtless about Samuel Esh, not to Kate. While she couldn't explain the purchase of the courting buggy, she could at least rest assured by the knowledge that he worked at an extra job in order to buy it.

For the next hour, the youth group sang songs from the Ausbund as well as other songs about God and faith. Kate preferred the songs from the Ausbund. She knew some of them by heart, and when the *vorsinger* began to sing one of her favorites, she smiled as she lifted up her voice to join the others.

Oh, you beloved brethren,
And sisters altogether,
Because we are all members
Of one body,

*So let us show loyalty
In loving one another,
Thereby God will be praised
In His throne on high.*

*For He, above all things,
Has commanded love,
Thereafter will we strive
At all times, early and late,
It does fulfill the law,
As is pointed out to us.
Therefore put on with desire
The virtues of Jesus Christ.*

—Ausbund, Song 119, verses 20–21

During the break, she slipped away from her friends and made her way into the main house to use the restroom.

"Is that Kate Zook?" An older woman greeted Kate with a warm smile, setting down her Bible on the sofa. She patted the seat next to her, indicating that Kate should join her. "I thought that was you when you came in."

Kate extended her hand to Jane King's *maem* before sitting down, feeling uncomfortable but knowing that she could not refuse the invitation to conversation.

"It's *gut* to see you out again, Kate."

"*Danke.*" She hated the constant reminders of the past few months of isolation. However, she knew it was to be expected. People were curious, even if the questions remained unspoken.

"How's your *maem* doing? She wasn't at church today."

"Taking care of David," Kate explained.

Jane entered the room from a doorway next to the stairs. She smiled when she saw Kate. "Kate Zook! I'm so glad to see you. Was hoping you'd be here tonight. I have two pie pans to return to your *maem*. Would you mind taking them?" She didn't wait for an answer as she hurried over to the counter to retrieve a small box. "It was right nice of her to send along the pies even though she didn't make it to worship today."

Kate took the box from Jane King, surprised to see some roots in the box, wrapped neatly in plastic bags. "What're these?"

"For your *maem*. Some butterfly bushes. I know how she loves to expand her garden with new roots."

Jane's *maem* raised an eyebrow. "Roots?"

"She keeps a garden out back," Kate explained. She felt uncomfortable talking about it. "Likes to collect roots from people and replant them."

Jane leaned over and placed her hand on her *maem*'s shoulder. "She started it after her boy, Jacob, died. The accident, Maem. Remember?"

Kate lowered her eyes, willing the conversation to change to something else . . . anything else besides the accident that had taken Jacob. "I best get going," she said, hoisting the box onto her lap as she stood up and headed to the door. "*Danke* for the roots. Maem will be pleased, I'm sure."

Outside, she leaned against the door for a moment, collecting her thoughts. Another reminder of how much her parents had lost was not something she needed. Twelve years and the pain was still raw. David's accident hadn't helped, reopening old wounds. She walked back toward the barn and set the box just outside the door. She'd collect it later, when they were leaving. As she stood up and turned to the door, she bumped into someone. In the darkness, she couldn't see who it was and quickly backed away, offering her apologies.

Ella paused and stared at her. For the briefest of moments, her eyes narrowed, as if angry with Kate. The reaction took Kate by surprise and she immediately apologized once again.

"I didn't see you there," she offered as her way of excuse. "Didn't mean to get in your way."

"Again," Ella retorted, a strange bitterness in her voice. "I shouldn't be surprised."

Kate frowned, wondering at Ella's response. *Again?* When had she ever gotten in Ella's way in the past? For the most part, her interactions with Ella were limited to worship service. There was no reason for such a response from her—unless . . . unless. The image of Ella's tormented face as she'd gazed at Samuel during volleyball recurred to Kate. Part of her wanted to inquire about Ella's well-being, but she felt too caught off guard to muster the courage to speak. Besides, Ella gave her no opportunity as she moved past her, walking toward the house.

She felt a hand on her shoulder and jumped, startled to see Samuel behind her. From the concerned look on his face, she knew that he had witnessed what just occurred.

"You all right?"

She nodded her head.

"Want to leave early? We can take a nice long drive." He glanced at the sky. "Stars are out and it's warm enough, *ja?*"

He carried the box to the buggy, securing it under the seat before he helped her step up and get situated. As he backed up the buggy, she saw a lone figure standing in the doorway of the house and, even without being able to see clearly, she knew it was Ella.

Samuel glanced at her. "You ignore her, Kate."

"I . . . I just don't understand."

He took a deep breath and remained silent, contemplating what to say in response. She waited patiently, allowing him the time to organize his thoughts. One of the reasons courting youths tended to keep their relationships secret was to avoid this very situation. It allowed couples to avoid embarrassment when relationships did not work out. Unfortunately, everyone had known about Ella and Samuel, and now everyone knew about Samuel and Kate. But perhaps his show of affection was nothing to count on. While she enjoyed his company and hoped for his favor, she also knew that nothing had been promised as far as a future. She, too, could be jilted. She only prayed that didn't happen.

"Kate, I don't want to speak poorly of anyone," Samuel finally said. "And things that happen between two people shouldn't be shared. I can't do that."

"I wouldn't expect you to do that."

He nodded his head, clearly appreciating her understanding. "Let's just leave it at this: there was a disagreement, and I feel a lot of regret that I didn't do what should have been done, *ja?*"

His cryptic explanation did little to illuminate the situation. However, she accepted his words as reason enough to maintain her confidence in Samuel as a godly man.

CHAPTER TWELVE

"You should invite him for supper," Maem said one night. Maem sat in the padded rocking chair, the wooden runners creaking on the floor, even though she had a rectangular hook rug underneath it. "Seems he's intent on spending time with you anyway. And not caring who knows about it."

She was crocheting a small baby blanket for one of Daed's nieces who had just given birth to her first baby, a boy. As usual, the birth of a child was met with joyous, if slightly restrained, fanfare. Maem liked to crochet pretty blankets for the babies, regardless of what time of year they were born.

Watching her *maem's* fingers fly, the yarn draped over one finger while her other hand held the crochet hook, Kate shrugged her shoulders. She sensed disapproval in Maem's voice.

Although Samuel was doing little to hide his special friendship with Kate, Kate was not quite ready to be so open about it. And certainly not around David. She wanted to avoid exposing Samuel to another one of David's outbursts. And despite his attention and considerate nature, she certainly did not want to presume that Samuel's friendship was far more than just that. Just seeing Ella at the youth gatherings was reminder enough that nothing was set in stone.

For the next few weeks, she noticed subtle changes in her life and, as a result, a different atmosphere at home. While nothing in her regular schedule had really changed, with the exception of Samuel driving her home from Susan's house each week, things felt different. She enjoyed those Saturday times together, when Samuel usually drove by way of winding side roads or stopped at a store where they could enjoy ice cream or a warm pretzel. For once in a very long time she felt happiness in her life.

Every Saturday without fail, he was there.

By the second week of May, Kate began to look forward to leaving Susan's house, fully expecting to see Samuel at the end of the lane waiting for her as she began walking home.

"Reckon I don't need the formalities of asking if you'd like a ride," he teased, a bouquet of wildflowers in his hand.

She blushed when he gave them to her.

"I packed a little basket. Thought we could go sit by the pond for a spell," he said as he helped her into his buggy.

"You packed a basket?" she asked, hiding her amusement at the image of him in the kitchen.

With a sheepish grin, he sat next to her and took up the reins. "Mayhaps my *maem* helped a bit," he admitted.

She laughed, feeling happier than she had in years. There was something so light and good about Samuel. Just being near him made her feel as if she didn't have a care in the world. During the short amount of time they were able to steal together, she absorbed his jovial nature and positive energy. His happiness was contagious, and she did all that she could to store it in her heart so that she could get through each week.

On Sundays, if there was a youth gathering after worship service, he arrived at her house in the late afternoon to take her in his buggy, and then each evening he brought her home. On the off Sundays, the weeks when they did not have a worship service, he arranged for something fun, usually with a group of other young people. Whether it was fishing or a simple picnic, Samuel always planned something to do so that he could spend time with Kate.

School let out in the third week of May. With Becca and Miriam home during the days, Kate felt as if she could breathe again. Maem now had three girls to share in her long list of chores, which gave Kate more time to spend in the garden in the late afternoons as well as the opportunity to begin visiting Verna on Monday afternoons.

As she was sitting near Verna on one of those occasions, her friend put into words the question that had long been in Kate's heart. "Do you ever wonder what happened between Samuel and Ella?"

Kate looked up from the quilt she was working on and stifled a gasp. "I'd never ask!" she said.

Verna laughed. "I didn't ask if you asked him. I asked if you wondered it."

Bending back over the quilt, Kate hesitated. She didn't want to lie, but admitting the truth seemed just as sinful. "I guess I can't say the thought hasn't crossed my mind," she finally acknowledged. "My friendship with him seemed to happen all of a sudden. I mean, I thought he would have married Ella by now." She set down her needle and stared at the wall. "I imagine that whatever occurred must have been upsetting on both sides."

"Whatever occurred, it happened right after Ruth died," Verna said.

Kate frowned. This was news indeed. "Really?" With the difference in age between Ella and Ruth as well as Samuel and David, she could hardly imagine what Ruth's untimely death might have to do with the end of Samuel and Ella's courtship. "Are you certain of that, Verna?"

Nodding her head, Verna continued. "*Ja*, right after the accident, they seemed to part ways. I don't know if anything was ever said. But I do know that he simply stopped going to singings for a while. She showed up, he didn't, and she went home with her *bruder*. That ended that." She reached over for the white yarn that they were using to knot-tie the quilt tops. "She seemed sad about it. Don't think she knows why he quit her."

For a moment, Kate stopped working. She wondered how she would feel if Samuel did the same thing to her. Certainly her heart would ache, but life would go on. Still, she felt sorrow for Ella. What little Kate knew about her was all positive, unlike some of the other young women who liked to smoke cigarettes or wear Englische clothes before they joined the church. Ella had a reputation for being a godly young woman. She had resisted the temptations of the non-Amish world and seemed poised to be a highly sought-after *fraa*.

"I imagine there is a reason," Kate sighed. "Might be best if it remain between the two of them."

Verna remained silent as she worked on the next knot tie. It gave Kate a break to wonder at the situation yet again. Did they simply stop getting along? Had Samuel hinted that he was unhappy? Had Ella done something that disagreed with him? During their time together, Kate never sensed anything amiss between her and Samuel. While he liked to laugh a lot, he also could be most serious at times. She found that she adapted well to his different moods, able to read them and respond accordingly. Still, the thought that he might unexpectedly quit her one day niggled her.

"Next Saturday, there's a group going to hike the Delaware Water Gap," Verna said. "You going?"

Her thoughts interrupted, Kate blinked and looked up. "Hiking?" She knew that once the planting was completed and the younger *kinner* were off school, the youth groups often planned day trips. Social outings were important to the development of lifelong

145

friendships. However, with her limited exposure to the outside world in the past few months, she hadn't heard about this trip.

"You should come. We'll have fun."

Kate's first thoughts were on David. Over the last few weeks, she had not spent as much of her free time at home. To leave on a fun day trip with the other youth would mean more of a burden on her Maem, even with Miriam and Becca at home to help. Plus, she was committed to help Susan on Saturdays.

"I don't think I could go," she said slowly. "I usually watch Susan's *boppli* anyway."

"Aw, you have a whole week to plan it. See if you can work something out." Verna lowered her voice so that no one in the house might overhear. "Besides, I heard Ella won't be going. She's gone visiting family in Sugar Creek for a few weeks."

"I hadn't heard that," Kate said. "I wonder why?"

Verna shrugged. "Seems someone might not be as happy as the rest of us about Samuel's attention being focused on you."

It took her two days to gather up the courage to speak to her *maem*. They were alone in the kitchen, David having retreated to his bedroom in a funk and the two girls outside playing with the kittens in the driveway. Kate kneaded a big ball of dough, flour up her arms to her elbows.

She hadn't planned to say anything. But she paused to glance out the window and saw a cardinal on the bird feeder. "How beautiful!" she said out loud.

"What is?"

Kate gestured toward the window. "Look. A cardinal. His red crest is so pretty."

Maem leaned over to get a better view. "That it is!"

Watching him for a few seconds, Kate wondered what magnificent birds might be spotted on the hike. Before she knew what she was saying, she blurted it out. "There's a hike on Saturday, Maem. I was wondering if I might be able to go."

"A hike?" Maem pinched at the dough and nodded her head, indicating that Kate could divide it into two loaves. "Who is organizing it?"

"I don't know," she admitted, feeling foolish for not having the answer. "But Verna invited me."

Maem raised an eyebrow.

"I told her I couldn't go, being that I help Susan on Saturdays," Kate quickly added. "Just seeing that cardinal made me think of it. I shouldn't have asked." She lowered her eyes and focused on the dough. "I'm sorry."

They worked in silence, Kate rolling the dough into loaves while Maem focused on the cheese curds that were cooling in the sink. When she drained the liquid, the sweet smell of whey rose into the air. Kate glanced over, watching as Maem used her fingers to break the curds into smaller pieces. Without being asked, Kate reached over for the jar of salt to hand to her *maem*.

Maem took the jar and, for a long moment, stared at it. Kate wondered at this strange reaction but did not question it.

"You have nothing to be sorry about," Maem finally said, a strange tone in her voice. "Find out more about this trip, and mayhaps Miriam can go help Susan instead." She set the jar of salt down on the counter and looked at Kate. There were tears welling in her eyes, tears that she refused to let fall as she smiled at her daughter. "You deserve a special day, Kate."

Kate looked away. She didn't feel as if she deserved a special day. She certainly didn't feel that she'd done anything worthy of such kind words from her *maem*. Swallowing what she wanted to say, Kate merely nodded her head. She didn't trust herself to speak, knowing that she'd say the wrong thing. It wasn't very often that she felt as though special consideration was bestowed upon her, not that she felt that she deserved it.

Later that afternoon, she walked over to Verna's and told her the good news. From Verna's reaction, Kate knew that her friend was excited to have Kate joining them for the hike at the Water Gap. She only wished that she felt the same anticipation and excitement. Instead of feeling any exhilaration for the adventure, she felt guilt as though she was abandoning both her parents and David. Still, in the deep recesses of her mind, she knew that this was exactly the type of social excursion that she needed. Even Maem had recognized that.

So, with all of her might, she tried to mirror Verna's reaction and share in her friend's delight . . . all the while worrying about how her parents would get through the day dealing with David without her help and assistance. Just the thought gave her a headache, one that permitted her to excuse herself from Verna's home to take the long and quiet fifteen-minute walk home by herself.

Chapter Thirteen

On the morning of the hike, the van arrived in her driveway at six thirty, right on time. She was not surprised to see John, Isaac, Hannah, and Esther already sitting in the back. Nor was she surprised to see Samuel. He motioned to her to come sit next to him, a warm smile on his face.

The group had hired two vans to transport the fourteen youths to the park, almost two and half hours away. The plan for the day included a two-mile hike by Hornbecks Creek to see the different waterfalls along the forested path. The drivers would pick up the group on the other end of the trail and take them south to Lenape Lake for their picnic lunch and more hiking.

Samuel tugged at the loose string to her prayer *kapp*. "Our first adventure," he whispered when she looked at him.

The same day that she had gone to Verna's to tell her the news, Samuel had stopped by to invite her to join the group. He'd caught up with her on the way back from the mailbox in the late afternoon.

"Kate!" he'd called out as he waved from the open door of his buggy. "Just the person I came to see!"

She hugged the mail to her chest and waited for him to catch up to her. Her bare feet felt dry and dusty. She wished she had worn her garden shoes.

"Wanted to ask you about Saturday," he said when he stopped the buggy. "Didn't know if you could get someone to fill in for you at your *aendi*'s. There's a hiking trip."

"Verna told me about it already," Kate replied.

"Oh?"

She nodded. "*Ja*, and Maem said I could go along."

He removed his hat and wiped his forehead with the back of his arm. "Does that mean you're courting Verna now?"

She laughed and shook her head.

"*Gut*! I'd hate to think you were two-timing me." He smiled back at her and winked. "You be certain to pack a nice big lunch, Kate. I want to sample your cooking for the first time at Lenape Lake!"

As he drove away, she had practically skipped down the drive-way toward the house. His sparkling eyes and gentle teasing made her heart skip a beat and her cheeks flush pink. It was a feeling she was getting used to . . . and liking it as well.

Now, as the van headed toward Route 222, she felt comfortable sitting next to Samuel and listening to him tease John about how his horse had come untied from the hitching post at the hardware store earlier in the week. As he told the story, he laughed and occasionally touched her shoulder. Each time he did that, she felt a warmth bloom on her skin under his fingers.

"I'm sure it's happened to you, Samuel," John shot back.

"*Nee*, John. I learned how to tie a safety knot that my horse can't undo!" He winked at Kate. "Mayhaps I could teach it to you?"

With the roads clear of traffic and the laughter in the van, the trip seemed to take no time at all to arrive at their initial drop-off point. By the time they pulled into the parking lot, Kate could hardly believe that two hours had passed. Between Samuel, John, and Isaac teasing one another, the other young women in the van had laughed during the entire journey. Kate was almost sorry that the ride was over when it was time to depart the van.

When they started hiking the trail, Kate was glad that she had worn her black sneakers rather than her boots. She wasn't partial to sneakers, but she gained a newfound appreciation for them as the group walked along the trail, especially as it became steep in some spots. For the first half hour, she walked with Verna, Sylvia, and Katie Ellen. They had ridden in the other van, so she hadn't a chance to visit with them during the drive. She noticed that Samuel and John walked ahead of the others, their heads tilted together as if they were deep in discussion.

The trees lined the path with a banner of green leaves. Birds chirped from the branches and squirrels scurried along the ground. When the path crossed open areas, Kate noticed wild honeysuckle bushes and inhaled the fragrant scent of the freshly blooming flowers.

By the time they reached the first waterfall, Kate felt more relaxed than she had in months. She stood alongside Verna, staring at the cascading water as it rained down the thirty-foot drop. The peaceful sound of the water added to her sense of calm. For a moment, she shut her eyes and just listened to the sounds of nature.

"You sense it, too?"

She opened her eyes and turned to look at Samuel. "Sense it?"

He placed his hand on her shoulder and looked at the water. "God's grace. It's here. We are surrounded by it, Kate."

Following his gaze, she stared at the gushing water. It fell over the rocks in a way that looked like soft white fabric fluttering in the wind from a clothesline. The waterfall was narrow at the top and wider at the bottom, with the underneath rocks visible in the middle.

"Only God could have created something so perfect," he sighed.

Kate looked at him, studying his profile. He didn't seem to mind, or perhaps he didn't notice, that she watched him. The serious look on his face as he admired the view caught her off guard and, once again, hinted at the many different layers to his personality. He continued to intrigue her, surprising her with the depth as well as breadth of his emotions.

When he finally glanced at her, he smiled and removed his hand from her shoulder. "Let's walk together, Kate," he said, his voice low. "The middle falls aren't that far from here, and I've shared you enough for a while."

They walked slowly, lagging behind the others. He picked up a stick from the ground, scratching at the bark with his fingernail. It peeled off in long sheets, which he dropped to the ground as if leaving a trail behind him.

"I like nature, Kate," he announced. "I thought about what you said a few weeks back, about treeless cities."

That surprised her. She hadn't thought she had said anything worthy of reflection.

"I'm glad I traveled," he continued. "Don't get me wrong. But I'm happiest right where I started. There's something about being a farmer that sure does keep me connected with God."

She pursed her lips, sensing that serious Samuel was at hand. "How so?"

"It's hard to explain." He took a few more steps, a pensive look on his face. She knew that he was seeking the way to describe what he felt. "God has given us a gift, Kate. He has made us the overseers to this magnificent planet." He opened his arms and gestured toward the woods. "Every tree, bird, flower, and field . . . God made them for us."

She listened intently, hearing the passion in his voice.

"But with such a grand gift comes great responsibility," he continued, punctuating his words by pointing his finger in the air. "We must take great care of this gift and respect it in His name. The same goes for people. We need to take care of each other." He dropped the stick on the ground. "I don't think the rest of the world has figured that out yet, Kate."

The sorrow in his voice surprised her. "Why do you say that, Samuel?"

"Why, those cities were once wide-open spaces! Instead of honoring God by working the land and taking care of this gift, man has destroyed it. Do you think God is happy with overdeveloped communities, where trees are torn down and people live on top of each other?" He shook his head. "*Nee*, He is not happy. Nor are the people."

"You think Englische people are unhappy?"

He shrugged. "I'm sure that they *think* they are happy, but in reality they are disconnected from each other and from our true purpose." The toe of his boot found the side of a rock, and he kicked it into the tall grass. "If we can't watch out for our neighbors, how can we be responsible for tending God's other creations?"

"It doesn't sound very promising when you put it like that."

He glanced at her with sad eyes. "*Nee*, it does not, Kate."

Just then, from overhead, a loud noise interrupted them. A bird called out from above. They both looked up and, after shielding their eyes from the bright sun, saw the wingspan of a large bird. Samuel caught his breath just as Kate recognized it.

"Is that a bald eagle?"

Samuel nodded. "*Ja*, I do believe it is! I saw the white head. And look at how large it is."

Just as quickly as they saw it, it disappeared over the tree line.

Kate dropped her arm and turned to face Samuel. "Think about the history of that bird," she said. "Look at what is around us right now." She gestured toward the woods. "We've managed to take good enough care of God's gift to keep this pure and untainted by the outside communities. Maybe there is hope for the rest of the world after all."

"Your positive outlook on life inspires me, Kate," he said, his voice low and soft. He glanced back in the direction where the eagle disappeared. "Mayhaps there is hope, indeed." The wistful look in his eyes told her that he wasn't talking about the eagle but about something else that weighed heavily on his mind.

By the time they caught up with the rest of the group at the next waterfall, Kate had almost forgotten that they were not alone. She almost wished they were. Samuel's attention to every detail of nature impressed her as did his extensive knowledge of birds and flora. He confided in her that he kept a collection of pressed flowers from his travels, each one carefully preserved between layers of wax paper in a bound book that he had made for that very purpose.

"And you recall where you picked every flower?" She was amazed at this new side of Samuel. *How sensitive of him*, she thought.

"I label each one," he admitted. "Where I found it, what I was doing, who I was with." He reached into his pocket and pulled out a white handkerchief. With great pride, he unfolded it and showed her a cluster of honeysuckles. "I'll be adding this to the collection, Kate, from our first adventure together."

For a split second, she wondered if there were any flowers pressed in the book from adventures he may have shared with Ella. Just as quickly, she pushed the thought away, knowing jealousy was a sin and immediately disliking herself for having felt it.

"I imagine your book is very pretty," she said, ashamed at her previous thoughts.

"Mayhaps I'll show it to you one day," he replied. Carefully, he refolded the handkerchief and gently slid it into the front pocket of his trousers.

Shortly after they had passed the third and final waterfall, the trail became steep with several trees blocking the path. Kate stood next to Verna and Sylvia as the men assessed the blowdown. Samuel was one of the first to climb over the trunks, avoiding the branches that created an obstacle course. He tried to break several of the thinner branches so that the young women could follow. Without any tools, the task was daunting. The tree was simply too large to properly clear.

"We can just walk around the roots," Esther called out.

Samuel and John stood on the other side. Kate could see Samuel frown, unhappy with that idea. When the other men made it across the downed trees, one of them agreed that it was too dangerous for the women. Esther didn't wait for more discussion. Instead, she started walking along the trunk of the tree, pushing through brambles and leading the way for the other women.

"Careful here," Esther called over her shoulder. "Ground's soft by the root ball."

Kate followed, her hand pressed against the trunk of the tree until she neared the roots. She looked up, amazed at how large they were, at least eight times the size of the tree's diameter. The dried dirt indicated that the trees had fallen a while ago, most likely during the winter. With so much snow and ice, it didn't surprise her. However, she couldn't help but wonder why there had been no signs at the beginning of the trail regarding the blowdowns that blocked the trail.

Just as she stepped behind Verna along the crevice, her foot slipped and she fell, tumbling down into a watery hole underneath the tree's exposed roots.

"Kate!"

When she heard Verna shout for her, Kate tried to sit up, but her hands felt only mud. It was cold and slippery. She managed to kneel and immediately felt a shooting pain in her right ankle. She heard more commotion and noise but could only register the fact that she was partially submerged in mud with a twisted ankle. She felt tears fill her eyes from both the pain and embarrassment at her clumsiness.

"I got you." Two hands lifted her by her arms, slipping underneath her to pull her out of the hole. Without looking, she knew it was Samuel.

"I'm so sorry," she whispered, avoiding the eyes of the women who crowded around her, trying to see if she was all right.

He pressed his lips together and knelt by her side, one hand under her head as he wiped the mud from her cheeks.

"You're a mess, Kate Zook!" he finally said. The lightness of his tone countered the concern in his eyes. "You hurt at all?"

She nodded her head, trying to hold herself together. "My ankle." Reaching her hand down, she realized that her dress was wet from muddy water. She fought the urge to cry, her humiliation increased by the knowledge that she was filthy dirty.

He let his fingers run along her lower leg, trying to feel if anything was broken. Gently, he removed her wet sneaker and black sock, resting her foot on his knee. "Can you wiggle your toes?"

Wishing that everyone would give her a moment to compose herself, she avoided looking at him and did as he instructed. "*Ja*, I can wiggle them," she said, then lowered her voice. "Does everyone have to stare so?"

He covered her bare toes with his hand, the warmth of his touch startling her. No one had ever before touched her bare skin. The intimacy of the gesture caused her to jump and she hoped that no one noticed.

"Mayhaps you could go wait over there," Samuel said to the young women nearby. "Give her a minute, *ja*?"

When they left, he released her foot and stood up, reaching a hand down to help her to stand. She leaned against his arm and tried to put weight on her right foot. A shooting pain ran up her leg and she winced.

"No good, eh?"

She shook her head.

He pursed his lips and glanced over at the group. They stood to the side, waiting and watching. "Well, we don't have much choice, do we? We can't go back, so we have to go forward."

Taking a deep breath, she nodded her head. "I can do it."

"I'll be right here by your side, Kate," he said. "Every step of the way this time."

She lifted her eyes, tears filling them, and looked at him. "I feel like such a burden," she said.

"Seems this is the second time I left you alone and you got hurt," he mumbled.

The pain in her ankle outweighed her curiosity at what he'd said. Rather than ask his meaning, she merely replied, "I should have watched where I was walking. It's my fault, Samuel. I'm so sorry."

Samuel didn't reply, a frown on his face as he supported her weight. She wondered if he was upset with her and didn't blame him if he was. After all, this was their first big adventure, and she'd twisted her ankle while in the middle of a hike through the woods. She could only imagine how disappointed he was. She'd surely ruined what was supposed to be a fun day of enjoying nature. Determined to not further wreck the day, she took a deep breath and did her best to walk beside him, ignoring the pain in her ankle and just focusing on taking one step at a time.

By the time they caught up with the others at the end of the trail, it was past noon and Kate apologized to the others for having kept them waiting. No amount of reassurance from her friends eliminated the disheartened feeling that grew in her chest. She did her best to not show how painful her ankle felt as they climbed into the vans for the short trip to the lake.

Only Samuel's occasional inquiries brought any attention to her injury. For the rest of the day, she sat quietly on a blanket in the shade of a tree by the lake, watching as the other youths continued hiking or ventured into the water, the men rolling up their pants while the women held the edge of their dresses so that they did not get wet.

Samuel did not join them. He seemed content to stay by Kate's side, lounging on the blanket and sharing more stories with her. She almost forgot about her injured ankle as he made her laugh, telling of his antics as a child and sharing details of how often he had been taken out to the woodshed by his *daed*, something that his younger brother Joshua had not escaped, either.

By the time the van drivers indicated they were ready for the long drive back, Kate felt as if the afternoon had not been ill spent, despite not being able to walk into the water or hike more trails. She sat next to Samuel on the ride home, drowsiness overcoming her, and without realizing it, she fell asleep with her head on his shoulder.

Chapter Fourteen

For the next week Kate stayed inside the house, her leg propped up on a stool so that her ankle could heal properly. Her morning chores were limited to folding the clean, dry clothes and mending tears in clothing. She complained that she felt useless, but Maem insisted that she relax, keeping the weight off her foot.

By Thursday she couldn't take any more sitting inside the house. She felt helpless, not being able to assist with the chores, gardening, or even taking care of David. She also noticed that the more attention she received from Maem, the more bitter he grew. His comments and remarks became more cutting and horrid to the point that Maem seemed to have him sitting outside for most of the day, despite his complaints that he was tired.

On Friday morning she made up her mind that enough was enough. The previous day she'd felt less pain when she walked. So she woke up extra early and dressed in the dark so that she could hurry downstairs before anyone else awoke. She was determined to help Daed with the morning milking.

It wasn't as though he had complained about milking the cows without her help. Kate just knew that it was a lot of work, and with only one set of hands, it took twice as long. Of course, Miriam and

Becca awoke at their regular time to help with the stall mucking and haying of the animals. Still, Kate felt obligated to help. She wasn't the kind of person to sit around and let others tend to her chores, injury or no injury.

When she opened the door to the dairy, she was surprised to see the kerosene lantern already lit in the barn. She hadn't heard Daed walk down the stairs when she was dressing, the creaking of that third step always a dead giveaway that it was time to awaken in the morning. But sure enough, the light was on and she could hear him talking to one of the cows.

"Daed? What time did you get up, then?" she called out, limping over to the side room to grab her stool and bucket.

"Is that you, Kate?"

She stopped and spun around, shocked to see Samuel stand up from behind the cow. "Samuel!"

He stood by the cow, a battered straw hat on his head. In his work clothes, he looked different than she was used to seeing him. Normally, he wore his clean Sunday outfit when he came calling for her. Not today. He wore his dirty black trousers with suspenders that crisscrossed in the back. His blue work shirt had seen better days. There was a hole in the sleeve near his shoulder. And when he walked around the cow to approach her, she noticed his boots were old and clunky.

But the grin on his face was pure Samuel.

"And *gut mariye* to you, Kate!" He acted as if his presence in the barn was nothing out of the ordinary.

Kate, however, felt stunned. "What on earth are you doing here?"

He raised an eyebrow and peered at her, that familiar sparkle in his blue eyes. "Mayhaps a better question is what *you* are doing here? A little bird told me that you're supposed to be off your feet for a week, ain't so?" He glanced around. "Being in here with a bucket in your hand, looking ready to milk cows, sure isn't recovering, now, is it?"

"Samuel!" She could hardly make sense of what she was seeing. Not only was Samuel milking the cows, he appeared more than comfortable doing so. She ignored his question by repeating her own. "Why are you here?"

"What does it look like, Kate?" He gestured toward the cows. "I'm helping your *daed*."

"At four thirty in the morning?" She almost laughed, especially given his even-natured tone. "Whatever for?"

He shrugged his shoulders, leaning against the metal post. "Figured your *daed* needed some help with the morning milking. Felt responsible for your injury."

Responsible? She wondered why he would feel responsible for her injury. And now, as a result, he was helping her *daed* each morning? She had a hard time understanding the motivation behind Samuel undertaking such a monumental inconvenience, especially when his help was certainly needed at his own *daed*'s farm.

"Have you been here all week, then?"

He nodded his head. "Sure have."

"Oh help," she muttered.

"Now, you march yourself right back inside and relax. Between your *daed* and I, we have everything covered out here. No need for you to be hobbling around, risking more injury, Kate." He dunked under the railing and took her elbow in his hand, gently guiding her back toward the house.

Speechless, she didn't argue as she followed his lead.

"Hey now," Daed said when Samuel walked into the kitchen. "What's this, then?"

Samuel shook his head as he guided her to the sofa. "Found a little mouse in the haystacks today, it seems."

To Kate's surprise, Daed laughed. She stared at him, her mouth dropping. When was the last time she had heard Daed laugh? Certainly not since David's accident.

"What's going on here?" she managed to ask. "I don't understand . . ."

Samuel shook his head at her. "Nothing to understand." He situated her on the sofa, and as if it were the most natural thing in the world, he propped up her foot on the stool. "Now you relax and work on healing. No reason to have that look on your face, Kate. I'm just helping out a spell. That's all."

But it was more than that. She could tell right away. Something had transpired between Samuel and her *daed*. The ease with which they communicated was something Kate had never before seen. And Samuel had told her he'd been coming to help Daed all week. Why had no one mentioned it to her?

She was still sitting on the sofa, stunned by this surprise revelation when Maem came down the stairs. She was pinning her prayer *kapp* as she entered the kitchen, a peaceful look on her face.

"Up already, then?"

"Maem, what's going on around here?"

Startled, Maem glanced around the kitchen, then looked back at Kate. She appeared genuinely perplexed. "Whatever do you mean? Nothing is going on."

"I just saw Samuel out in the dairy!"

Maem frowned. "What were you doing out there, Kate? You know you aren't supposed to be putting weight on your ankle."

Kate sighed, exasperated. "That's not the point."

Maem headed toward the sink, reaching for the kettle of water to begin preparing coffee. That was always the first order of the day. "What is your point, Kate?"

A laugh almost escaped from her lips. "Why is Samuel here? Everyone is acting like it's the most natural thing in the world . . . having Samuel helping Daed with my chores!"

"I think it's rather kind of him to have offered," Maem said, setting the kettle on the stove. She fiddled with the dial until the familiar poof of propane caught and a flame flickered under the pot. "He showed up and spoke to your *daed*, insisting to help while you are recuperating. He's quite a nice young man, isn't he?"

In disbelief, Kate shook her head. "Why didn't anyone tell me?"

"Why should anyone have told you?" Maem countered, an odd expression on her face. Kate squirmed under her *maem's* scrutiny. "Doesn't involve you, does it now?"

Tossing her hands in the air, Kate sank back into the sofa. She had no idea why they had been so secretive about Samuel being at the farm. No one had mentioned a word. She made a mental note to corner Miriam later, see if she had known about Samuel's help in the dairy.

To her surprise, Miriam knew nothing about it. She professed innocence and seemed genuinely as surprised as Kate. They both knew better than to question Becca. From what Kate could best figure, Samuel arrived at four to start the milking and helped her *daed* until five thirty, when he returned to his own family's farm for morning chores. Under the cloak of dawn's darkness, Samuel Esh had been both arriving and leaving, with no one besides Maem and Daed being any the wiser.

"Oh, Kate," Miriam whispered happily. "Do you think this means . . . ?"

Kate grabbed Miriam's hands, holding them before her. "Shh! Don't even say it, Miriam! It means nothing more than a very nice young man helping Daed."

"He must be very nice to get up an extra hour early to get here by four o'clock!" Miriam said, her voice dripping with sarcasm. "I'd say he's *ferhoodled* for sure and certain! I hope Maem planted plenty of celery."

Shaking her head, Kate tried to change the subject. "He's helping Daed, not me. People do it all the time."

As the day wore on, even Becca seemed to catch the scent of romance in the air. Despite not knowing about Samuel's mornings at their farm, she sensed something was happening. When she came in from weeding the garden, she plopped on the sofa next to Kate and looked at her.

"You need to get better fast, Kate," she said, plucking at the dirt on her bare knee. "Getting tired of doing all your chores."

"Becca!" Maem scolded. Miriam was helping her make shoofly pies at the counter. Clearly, they had both overheard Becca's comment.

"It's true!" Becca shot back. "She hurts her foot and the whole world shifts around her!" Huffing, she crossed her arms over her chest and pouted. "It's as if she's already married and not here anymore!"

Kate's mouth dropped open, and she fought the urge to respond. Out of the corner of her eye, she caught Miriam smiling while she pressed the pie dough into the pans. It was Maem who jumped to her defense.

"Becca, you just leave your *schwester* alone, now!"

"Special treatment, I say," Becca mumbled.

Maem gestured toward the door. "Go help your Daed with the evening milking. See if some good hard work cures you of complaining."

"Aw, Maem!" But knowing better than to argue further, Becca stood up and walked back to the door, her feet dragging on the linoleum as she went. "Not fair," she grumbled just loud enough for everyone to hear before she shoved open the screen door.

"That girl," Maem said, exasperated and worn out. "The day that one gets married, I don't think I'll be none too sad to see her go. Surprised that someone might want to marry her, mayhaps, but not sad to hand her over to someone else for a while!"

Miriam giggled.

Kate, however, remained quiet as she sat on the sofa. Her mind whirled in twenty directions as she pondered Samuel's intentions. None of this made sense to her. From what she knew, he'd courted Ella for almost eight months. Yet that had ended.

She found joy in his attentions, but there was still that seed of doubt, planted deep in the pit of her stomach that she would disappoint him. And that he would move on yet again. He didn't know about her role in David's accident, after all. Nor did he know about Jacob.

Staring out the window, Kate felt her heart beat rapidly as she realized that she needed to talk to him, to set the matter straight. A special friendship built on a weak foundation would never last. And she felt as if the weight of her sins needed to be aired. Then, at least, he would know the truth and could decide on his own whether he felt she was still a worthy partner for the future.

Chapter Fifteen

By the weekend, Kate managed to convince her parents that her ankle was healed enough to help with chores. She even managed to attend the worship service, although she had a hard time during the two kneeling prayers.

After worship, her *daed* indicated that they would not stay for fellowship. Her older brother, Thomas, was going to visit in the afternoon and because Maem stayed behind once again for David, Daed didn't want to linger over the dinner meal.

For the first time in a long while, Kate felt the loss keenly of returning home and missing the chance to visit with her friends while helping to serve the fellowship meal. Now that she was back in the routine of socializing a bit, she realized how much she had missed them during her months of isolation after the accident.

But thanks to Samuel, her perspective had changed. She felt an increased ability to attend gatherings and reconnect with her friends. It was his encouragement that made her feel confident to do so.

She knew that she had a lot to be grateful for because of Samuel. During the course of her life, she'd rarely interacted with any men outside of her family. Yet Samuel had managed to draw her out of her shell and into conversations that she never would have considered discussing before. No topic seemed off-limits for him, whether it was Amish traditions, Englische technology, or Christian theology.

Kate had come to eagerly anticipate her buggy rides with Samuel, the only time they truly spent alone. Now, however, the burden of confiding in him, and telling him the truth, weighed on her mind. She worried over his reaction.

When they returned from worship service, Maem sat on the porch with David, enjoying the breeze and the birds. The impatiens she had planted in May bloomed large and colorful along the walkway with black-eyed Susans surrounding the base of the house. She rested her head on the back of the rocking chair, her eyes shut as she gently rocked back and forth, a peaceful expression on her face.

David presented a different picture. Instead of enjoying the fresh air or seeming thankful for Maem's sacrifice in missing worship service on his behalf, David sat in his wheelchair, his head resting on his elbow as he scowled, looking into the distance angrily.

Just the week before, Daed had hung three bird feeders from the tree near the porch. Despite wanting the birds to eat bugs, he filled them with different types of feed to attract as many birds as he could. Maem had set her bird book on the bench where David could reach it to identify the different types of birds. From the looks of it, he had never so much as opened it.

Kate didn't need to ask why David's mood was so foul. Without doubt, she suspected that Thomas's pending arrival bothered him. Five years older than David, Thomas was mature enough to see through his younger brother's anger. In the past, Thomas had gone so far as to refuse to tolerate David's insolence. On more than one occasion, he had even interrupted the visit to abruptly leave with his wife.

"No need to be poisoned by such malice," he had explained before leaving.

Kate never blamed him. The tense relationship between Thomas and David went back at least ten years, perhaps longer. Kate couldn't remember when it had started and she certainly had no idea as to why. By the look on David's face, his brow so deeply furrowed in indignation, she suspected the afternoon would not end well.

"Home already, then?" Maem said when she opened her eyes, Becca's laughter having awakened her. "I didn't realize it was so late. Need to set the table."

"I can do it, Maem," Kate offered. "You relax a spell."

Inside the kitchen, the smell of home-cooked food filled the room. The meal had been prepared the previous day so that Maem wouldn't have to work on the Lord's Day. But everything smelled delicious: they'd be eating ham and scalloped potatoes. The rolls were neatly arranged in a basket and covered with a napkin. Bowls of applesauce, canned beets, and coleslaw were set out in dishes, too, and covered with pot lids to keep away flies.

Quickly, Kate covered the table with a plain white cloth and began to place the plates in front of each chair and along the bench where she sat with Miriam and Becca. Eight plate settings for their family surrounded the table, plus a high chair for baby Stephen. Soon, however, there would be a new addition. Linda was expecting a second child in August, almost a year to the day after Stephen had been born.

"Did you set everything, then?" Maem said as she came inside, hurrying to the sink to wash her hands.

"You put out an extra setting."

"I did?" Maem paused and recounted the places at the table. "No, I didn't."

"Eight adults, Maem. Susan doesn't live here anymore."

But Maem shook her head. "*Nee*, Kate. There are nine adults for supper tonight." Without hesitation, she picked up the extra plate and utensils, setting them on the side of the table with the bench. "You best go change your dress, Kate. Thomas should be here within the next hour." She glanced at the clock. "Or sooner, I reckon."

Upstairs in her room, Kate wondered who else was joining the family. Was Susan coming on her own? It seemed unlikely she'd leave her husband and the *boppli* at home. She quickly removed her white organza apron and cape, carefully hanging them on a hanger. Every Saturday night, she carefully ironed them so that there were no creases or wrinkles. She knew far too well that the older women watched with a critical eye to see which young woman would arrive with anything less than a perfectly crisp covering. She removed her black apron from the hanger and slipped it over her dark-blue dress, pausing to replace the hanger on the hook behind her door.

She wondered if Samuel was planning to fetch her for the singing. With Thomas and Linda visiting, she doubted she'd be permitted to attend. Her expression must have given away what she felt when she returned to the kitchen, for David immediately sensed her melancholy.

"What's bothering you?" David said, his tone needling. "Didn't get to see your boyfriend yesterday or today?"

Kate clenched her jaw and refused to take the bait. Everyone in the family seemed happy with Samuel's attention to Kate, with the exception of one person: David. He did nothing to hide how visibly unhappy he was with this relationship. The happier everyone else seemed, the more miserable he became.

It was true that she hadn't seen Samuel on Saturday. The previous day, Kate had not been able to help Susan. Instead, Miriam went in her place since Daed needed Kate's help with the first hay cutting. Even Becca had to assist, something that had not passed without complaint. Without a reason to go to Susan's house, there had been no Saturday buggy ride home with Samuel.

"That's enough, David," Maem reprimanded.

Kate tried to think back to when Thomas courted Linda. Like most Amish courtships, his had remained cloaked in secrecy until the bishop announced her *bruder*'s intentions at worship service. Kate suspected that, prior to that public announcement, Thomas confided in their parents. But for the rest of the family, his engagement had truly been a surprise.

That meant there was no teasing or ribbing from anyone. Of course, that was only right, as Thomas was quite serious in nature. He worked hard, saved his money. Six months before he married Linda, he had purchased a farm in Ephrata, which was not close enough for him to visit frequently. But Kate admired the way he always seemed to make plans and see them through.

Shortly after one thirty, Kate heard the arrival of a buggy, the gentle humming of the wheels and familiar clip-clop of the horse's hooves approaching the house, indicating that Thomas had finally arrived. Eager to escape the tension in the kitchen, she hurried outside to greet her brother and his wife.

"Why look at you!" Kate gushed, greeting Linda with a warm embrace. When they separated, she let her hands fall to Linda's enlarged belly. "My goodness! I think you have a watermelon under there."

Linda laughed. "Feels like it at times, too!"

Thomas walked around the side of the buggy, carrying their son, Stephen. At ten months of age, he was a big boy and already walking, although Kate quickly learned that he fell once for every three steps he took. She reached out to take him in her arms, snuggling him against her chest and nuzzling his neck until he giggled.

"Things look right *gut* around here," Thomas said, assessing the farm with an approving eye. "You holding up all right, then, Kate?"

She swung Stephen so that he sat on her hip, jiggling him just enough to keep him moving and happy. "We're holding up," she responded. "Everyone's pulling their weight."

"Everyone?" he asked, one eyebrow arched as he questioned her.

She merely responded with a gentle lifting of her shoulders.

Thomas pursed his lips, stealing a quick glance in Linda's direction. Kate recognized the look as the unspoken communication that only a husband and wife could share. Without being privy to their private conversations, Kate suspected she understood the meaning of their secret exchange. Clearly, Thomas was mentally preparing himself for dealing with David.

No sooner had they entered the house than Maem came bustling up from the cellar to greet them. She gushed over Stephen, quickly setting down the jars of chowchow she had brought upstairs so that she could pick him up and fuss. After all, he was her first grandchild.

"And you're feeling well, Linda?" she asked once the initial excitement of seeing Stephen calmed down. "You look well."

Truth was that she looked healthy enough but tired. Working on a farm with one small baby and another on the way was hard work. Kate didn't need to be told that. She knew that Linda surely had a few tough years ahead of her, especially if she had more babies right away. But like most Amish women, especially those who worked on farms, raising children was a blessing that Linda celebrated as a gift from God. There would be no complaints.

The good news was that Linda's family lived close enough to help her tend the *kinner*. Linda's younger sister had even stayed with them to help after Stephen was born. Kate suspected that the same would happen this time around, too.

David remained in the sunroom off the kitchen, his wheelchair facing the window. Rather than greet his brother, he continued staring outside, waiting for Thomas to approach him. Kate watched with curiosity as Thomas sat beside David, attempting to converse with him but getting little response.

While disappointed, more for Thomas's sake than David's, Kate knew she shouldn't have been surprised. After all, David rarely spoke anymore, except to complain or demand something. Daed seemed to stay outside more and more, avoiding confrontations with his son while Miriam and Becca escaped his wrath by helping Daed.

As always, it seemed that Kate bore the brunt of his anger.

The sound of Daed walking into the house caught her attention. He was speaking with someone and laughing as she heard the sound of his boots on the porch. Shifting to the side, she tried to peer out the window to see who he spoke to, but they were already inside the house.

Thomas stood up, leaving David's side as he called out, "Samuel Esh!" With a broad smile, Thomas crossed the room to greet Samuel as he entered the kitchen through the mudroom. "Been a while, my friend!"

Kate's mouth opened, and she lifted her hand to her hair as if to smooth back any stray strands. Becca caught her in the act and giggled, darting out of Miriam's way just in time to miss being pinched.

"Your *daed* mentioned you were stopping by this Sunday. Invited me over to visit a spell," Samuel said as he shook Thomas's hand. He greeted Linda and Maem before turning toward Kate. "Why hello, Kate Zook! Long time no see," he said with a smile and wink.

From behind her, she heard David scoff. Samuel's eyes flickered over her head in her brother's direction, but he remained smiling, his attention clearly on Kate.

She wondered why neither Maem nor Daed mentioned that Samuel had been invited. Of course, she remembered Maem suggesting that Kate invite him for supper. She hadn't, mostly because of David. Certainly Daed had extended the invitation as a way to thank Samuel for helping out while Kate recovered from her twisted ankle. Still, the secrecy concerned her. Why would they neglect to tell her?

She helped her *maem* finish preparing the afternoon meal by pouring fresh meadow tea into glasses and setting them at each place setting. Her heart pounded while she tried to listen to Thomas and Samuel's conversation, which was mainly about farming. Daed chimed in from time to time but seemed perfectly content to let his older son converse with their guest.

"Corn crop's growing nicely and we already have a second hay ready to cut next week. Growing fast this year," Thomas said. He reached up and took Stephen from his wife. "Might get five cuttings if the weather stays this way."

Daed nodded, impressed. "You must have good soil, then."

"With the prices of hay so high, I'm grateful to be able to sell some this year," Thomas added. "The extra income sure will come in helpful. Had a tough year last." He glanced at his *daed* and raised an eyebrow. "You managing all right, then?"

"Right as rain," Daed chirped cheerfully.

Kate paused what she was doing and looked up. *Right as rain?* That was Maem's expression and something she had never before heard Daed say. Ever since December, her *daed* had been quiet and forlorn, barely speaking and never laughing. Suddenly, he seemed like a new man, as if he had not one care in the world.

"In fact," Daed continued, "I've arranged to hire Samuel. He's going to help with some of the baling and harvesting."

She looked at Samuel, sitting in the chair beside Daed. They appeared completely at ease with each other. While she knew that her *daed* thought highly of Samuel, their new level of closeness still surprised her. Of course, the fact that Samuel offered to help Daed when she was injured must have cemented the budding friendship between them. To hear that Samuel would work the farm that summer and fall took her by surprise. Another private deal that no one had told her about. While she was pleased for Daed, and secretly glad to know that she'd be able to spend more time with Samuel, she wondered why no one had spoken of this new arrangement before now.

And then she caught sight of David, glaring at Samuel, and Kate knew. She knew why no one had discussed the agreement. She understood the unspoken dynamics of what was happening. Immediately, she felt sick to her stomach, an ache at her very core. For as much as David blamed Kate for his situation, his hatred was twice as deep for Samuel, not just for the incident with the Scrabble game but for now having replaced him as a working hand on the farm.

As if reading her mind, Thomas turned to his brother, addressing his question to David. "What about you, David? Seems about time for you to start helping in the barn."

Inwardly, Kate groaned. *Not this again*, she thought. The last visit from Thomas and Linda started well enough until the focus of the discussion had shifted to David. When Thomas had learned that his brother refused to attend any physical therapy, an argument had ensued. As always, Thomas had reprimanded him about not trying harder to accept and adapt to his disability; David merely responded with his typical outrage.

"Not much good for anything now, am I?" David snapped.

Shaking his head, Thomas shifted Stephen in his arms where the baby slept. "Seems there's a lot you could do to be useful," he started. "Still avoiding physical therapy?"

David looked away.

"I thought so," Thomas mumbled. "You're young, David, and still have a life ahead of you. It's a mistake to throw it away and not try."

Kate caught her breath and backed up so that she leaned against the counter. With all of her might, she willed Thomas to stop. *Please*, she prayed. *No ugliness today. No words. No arguments. No disputes in front of Samuel.*

To her relief, David did not respond. Instead, he continued staring out the window. Still, she felt embarrassed that Samuel had witnessed yet one more altercation with David.

Shortly after two o'clock, Maem called everyone to the table. Kate sat in her usual place next to Miriam, and to her surprise, Samuel took the seat next to her. His leg brushed against hers and she moved aside, giving him more room. She thought she saw him smile, just a little, when she did so. Becca took her place at the far end of the bench and across from David. It was a small table but everyone fit, despite being a little cramped.

When the before-prayer was finished and the plates began to be passed, Thomas looked up and addressed Kate. "I heard you hurt yourself just weekend last."

She nodded, taking the plate of warm ham from Miriam. "My ankle, *ja*."

"Hiking, I heard?"

Samuel chimed in, answering the question for her. "That's right. Up at the Water Gap. Lots of trees felled, from the winter storms, I reckon. Wasn't cleaned up yet." He glanced at Kate. "But she was a real trooper. Not one complaint about her injury," he said, pride in his eyes. "And I'm sure that hurt plenty."

"Doesn't surprise me. She's always been a tough one," Thomas added. He lifted his fork to his mouth but paused before eating. "Sometimes I wonder that she bears one too many burdens for those shoulders."

The compliments as well as the attention embarrassed her. Lowering her eyes, she knew that her cheeks were red because of the warmth she felt there.

Without any warning, David pushed back his wheelchair from the table. His narrowed eyes glowered as he glared in her direction.

"David," Maem said, her voice emotionless but firm. "We have not finished the meal."

"I've finished my meal," he snapped. "I've lost any appetite with this foolish rubbish." He started to maneuver the wheelchair toward his bedroom.

Samuel straightened his back. From the corner of her eyes, Kate saw the muscles twitch in his jaw. He clenched his teeth and pressed his lips together but remained silent.

"You have not been excused," Daed said. If the assertive tone of his voice didn't stop David, the stern look on Daed's face should have. "You will wait until we finish eating and say the after-prayer."

David remained defiant, refusing to return to the table. His eyes flickered toward Kate first and then to Thomas. "You think she bears too many burdens, do you?" He laughed, but it held no mirth. "I'd think you'd be the first one to know that she has caused many more burdens than she bears, Thomas. If she has any troublesome weight on her shoulders, it was caused by her own doing!"

"David!" Maem started to stand. "That's enough!"

Thomas, however, reached out to touch her arm. "Let him go, Maem," he said softly. "You can't fix ungrateful." He lifted his eyes and stared across the table at his brother. *"Therefore I will not refrain my mouth; I will speak in the anguish of my spirit; I will complain in the bitterness of my soul."*

At this comment, David bristled. "Bitterness? Is that what you think?"

Thomas remained calm, despite the anger in David's reaction. "What I see is what I speak. *And let the peace of Christ rule in your hearts, to which indeed you were called in one body. And be thankful.*"

"Thankful?" David spat out the word as if it tasted of poison. He turned his chair so that he faced the table. "What exactly is there to be *thankful* about?" He smacked the sides of his wheelchair with his hands. "This? A life in this chair?"

"You lived, David." Thomas spoke with no emotion in his voice. "And you can continue living a life that is fulfilling and good. That is what God wants. It is His will."

"I lived?" Once again, David laughed. "You call this living?" Lifting his chin, he shook his head. "I'd rather have died alongside Ruth." He paused and narrowed his eyes once again. "Or even Jacob!"

Under the table, Miriam grabbed Kate's hand as Maem gasped, "David, you don't know what you are saying!"

Smacking his hand on the tabletop, Daed demanded David's attention. "'*For I know the plans I have for you,*' declares the Lord, '*plans to prosper you and not to harm you, plans to give you hope and a future.*' You will not question God's plans in my house!"

Another laugh. "Hope? A future?"

"David, please . . ." Kate dared to plead.

"And you!" David turned his wrath in her direction. He stared at her, glowering with a raw expression of rage that frightened her. Never in her life had she ever seen such fury on anyone's face. "You were there that night! You knew!"

His words felt like a knife to her heart. She cringed, shutting her eyes as she tried to extract her hand from Miriam's. Miriam refused to let go. Instead, she squeezed Kate's hand even harder. On the other side of her, she felt Samuel flex his shoulders, stiffening at the words that David flung in her direction.

"You could have stopped it!"

Kate shook her head, her eyes still shut. *Make him stop*, she prayed. *Please, dear Lord, make him stop.*

"Like you could have stopped Jacob!"

"Stop . . ." she whispered.

"Instead, your life continues and you've moved along as if nothing has happened. Nothing to me. Nothing to Ruth. And nothing to Jacob!" He lifted his hand and pointed at her. "You, Kate, with shoulders bearing such burdens." She cringed at the sarcasm in his voice. "You live life despite the trail of casualties you leave in your wake."

"That's not fair," she said, opening her eyes and staring at him. How could he mention Jacob? How could he bring up that painful moment from so many years ago?

"None of this is fair!" he shouted back at her, once again gesturing toward his wheelchair.

The tears came to her eyes. "You know that I tried to tell you . . . to stop you . . ." She felt a hand on her knee and, to her horror, realized it was Samuel. For a moment, she had forgotten that he sat beside her. He had heard David's accusations, had heard what horrid things David said. While she had already decided to share the truth about that night with Samuel, Kate now realized that David had stolen that opportunity from her.

Her thoughts were interrupted when Daed stood up, his chair falling backward and rattling on the floor. "Enough!" He boomed. "I've heard enough!" He took a deep breath, making an attempt to calm down before he spoke again. "We must each appear before the judgment seat of Christ and take accord for our own actions." He directed these words toward David. "You blame Kate as Adam blamed Eve. God did not accept that," he said. "And neither will I. Not in this house!"

A silence fell over the room and David lowered his eyes. The unspoken threat of being banished quieted his temper. Kate, however, felt a lump growing in her throat and tears threatening to fall from her eyes.

He blames me. While she had known David harbored anger against her, she hadn't truly understood why. Now, as she felt the depth of his hatred, it became clear: He accepted no responsibility for the bad decision he had made in drinking before the accident. Instead, he'd shifted all of the blame onto her.

At this realization, her chest tightened and she felt light-headed. It was one thing to blame herself for not having spoken up. It was quite another thing to hear that he, too, blamed her.

God can help you rise above your mistakes. Wasn't that what her *maem* had always told her? After all, Scripture stated that faith was the substance of all things hoped for and the evidence of things not seen. Now, just as she was releasing her guilt regarding her unspoken knowledge regarding David's tendency toward alcohol, he outright accused her of being to blame?

The recrimination stung, bringing back all of those negative feelings and questions of faith with which she struggled for so long. Despite her *daed*'s reminder that David must take culpability for his own actions, Kate understood that she, too, would one day stand before Jesus and be judged.

The weight of that knowledge lay heavily on her shoulders. Unable to finish her meal, she folded her hands and laid them in her lap. She refused to look at anyone and couldn't wait for the meal to finally end. As soon as the after-prayer was said, she stood up and immediately began to clear the table, knowing that moving around and staying busy was the only thing that could keep her from weeping.

The tension in the air lingered long after David left the room. Kate stayed tucked in the corner of the kitchen, her mind focused on David's harsh words and the memory of the hurtful expression on his face. His words kept ringing in her ears. She wiped at her eyes, glad that no one could see the tears that escaped and fell down her cheek as she washed the dishes and set them aside.

At four o'clock, with a forty-five-minute ride ahead of them, Thomas and Linda prepared to leave. He was going to be late for the evening milking. Linda packed up her basket of things before taking Stephen from Miriam and following her husband outside. Samuel lingered behind while the others joined them to say their good-byes.

She felt him approach her. He hesitated, just for a moment, before he touched her arm and gently turned her so that she faced him. "Kate," he started. "What David said . . ."

Kate shook her head, swallowing as she tried to stop him from saying anything else. "Don't," she managed to whisper. "Please just don't say anything."

"I want you to know that I don't believe anything that he said."

Kate shut her eyes and bit her lower lip. *Now*, she told herself. *It's now or never.* "But he spoke the truth, Samuel," she blurted out, opening her eyes to look at him. It was painful to see his reaction. "What he said is all true."

"I don't understand," he said, his blue eyes searching hers.

Fighting tears, Kate nodded her head. "It's true. It's my fault that my brother Jacob died. And it's my fault that David got into an accident." She choked back a sob and wiped at her tears with the palm of her hand. "I'm a sinner, Samuel. Plain and simple. I wanted to tell you myself. I planned to anyway."

"A sinner?" Samuel repeated the word, disbelief in his voice.

"I don't know how to tell you this," she heard herself say. "But I'm thinking I shouldn't be accepting no more rides with you, Samuel."

He blinked at her announcement.

"I . . . I'm not ungrateful for your rides and all," she stammered. "And we sure do have nice conversations. I've enjoyed the fishing and the hiking and the picnic . . ."

He raised an eyebrow. His silence encouraged her to continue.

"But I best not be misleading you none." She shook her head, as if convincing herself. "*Nee*, that's the truth, Samuel. You are a *gut* man and have a right *gut* reputation. It wouldn't do you any good to be seen courting someone like me."

"I see," was all he managed to say.

The door opened to the mudroom and she could hear her parents, talking softly between each other before they entered the kitchen. Kate turned around, ashamed at herself for having cried in front of Samuel. With her back turned, she didn't have to face her parents or Samuel.

"Everything all right, then?" she heard her *daed* ask.

Samuel sounded upbeat when he responded, but Kate detected a hint of heartache in his voice. "*Ja*, of course," he said. "But I reckon I best be headed out anyway. Daed will need my help with chores, too." Kate heard him crossing the floor, slowly, toward her parents, and she glanced over her shoulder in time to see him shake their hands. "Sure do thank you for supper," he said.

Daed mumbled something, too low for Kate to hear; she suspected it was an apology for David's outburst.

Before Samuel left, he paused at the door and turned, observing Kate for a long moment. When she realized that he was watching her and lifted her eyes to meet his, he forced a weak smile. "See you later, then?"

Kate turned her gaze away from him, the slight shake of her head meant to indicate otherwise.

She stood there, leaning against the counter with her arms crossed over her chest long after the sound of his horse and buggy disappeared down the road. Frozen in place, she rehashed the events of the evening, knowing that it was for the best that Samuel knew and could make his own informed decision. Still, the pain in her heart was more terrible than she'd expected. Without Samuel, her future looked as bleak as David's.

CHAPTER SIXTEEN

The following week, Kate felt invisible. She worked at her regular time and went through the motions of her chores. But her heart was no longer joyful. Gone were her smiles and cheerful nature. Silence followed her as she milked the cows, weeded the garden, and helped her *maem* in the kitchen.

At first, her silence was met with respect and understanding. When her appetite disappeared, however, Maem began to show an abundance of concern.

"You've barely touched your plate, Kate," she scolded one night.

Kate lifted her shoulders in an apologetic shrug. What could she do? Hunger evaded her. What little she did eat seemed to sit in her stomach like a rock that caused pain. Food was tasteless. Colors were flat. Sounds, merely background noise.

Every night, immediately after supper, she excused herself and retreated to her room where, for an hour, she knelt beside the bed, her hands folded and her head tipped in prayer. Despite knowing she was already forgiven by God, she found it hard to believe. She prayed for the strength to accept the forgiveness afforded by God. The harder she prayed, the more despondent she felt.

David, however, seemed to take satisfaction in Kate's silent show of melancholy.

As much as possible, her parents tried to find ways to keep the two of them separated, knowing that David fed off her sorrow. Kate heard them whispering outside her door, trying to figure out what to do. Since David was not a baptized member of the church, they could not get the bishop or deacons involved. His handicap limited them in putting him out of the house, which they didn't want to do as such a decision felt unchristian. Yet they knew that something had to be done.

On Friday and Saturday, Kate helped her *daed* with a hay cutting, spending the majority of her day outdoors in the sun. With no rain in the forecast, the hay needed to be cut and raked so that it could dry for a few days before baling. Any moisture in the bales could cause composting, which had been known to ignite and cause barn fires. Seasoned farmers knew to wait before baling, while younger farmers often learned the hard way.

By Sunday afternoon, Kate felt exhausted and stayed in bed, claiming aches in both her head and her body. To her relief, Maem left her alone, checking in on her only twice with fresh water and some frozen soup that she'd reheated on the stove.

By evening, as the sun dipped over the horizon, Miriam rapped twice on the door before poking her head inside. "You awake?"

Kate sat up in bed. "*Ja*, I am."

Without being invited, Miriam slipped inside and shut the door behind herself. "Feeling any better, then?"

Kate shook her head.

"Mayhaps this will help, I don't know," Miriam said, her eyes showing her concern for Kate. "But Samuel was here earlier."

Kate shut her eyes and leaned her head against the headboard of her bed. "Whatever for?" And then she remembered that Daed had hired Samuel to help with baling hay that next week. She groaned and sank down under her covers. "Why did Daed have to hire him?"

Sitting down on the mattress at the foot of the bed, Miriam curled up, her legs tucked under her as she stared at her older sister. "Kate, I thought you cared for Samuel," she said, an expression of confused curiosity on her face.

"It's not that easy, Miriam," Kate responded. "There are things you just can't understand."

"Like what?" Miriam wasn't about to give up easily. "Explain them to me."

Sighing, Kate looked at her sister. She was almost fourteen, and in two years, young men would be able to court her. *Perhaps*, she thought, *Miriam needs to learn the significance of choices made for our future.*

"Samuel is a *gut* man," she started. "He has a *wunderbar* reputation and will make a fine husband to a godly and righteous woman, Miriam."

Miriam nodded her head in agreement.

"That woman is not me."

At this, Miriam looked surprised. "Why not?"

Kate sighed and pulled her knees up, wrapping her arms around them. "I do care for Samuel, Miriam. But I care enough about him to know that he needs a woman who is better than I am. Besides, Maem and Daed need my help with David. If I married and moved away, that would put an undue burden on you and Becca. It's not your fault that David is bound to the wheelchair and can't help. Your future shouldn't be affected."

"And yours should?"

Kate wanted to tell Miriam the truth. She wanted to share about David being drunk, a sinner aligned with Satan over whiskey. But to admit that would be slanderous against both him and Ruth, for surely she had been drinking, too. Or, if not, she knew David had been.

And then would come the questions about how Kate had known David drank and didn't tell anyone. Kate would have to confess to her sister that she had refused to get in the buggy, and allowed Ruth to ride to her death beside her intoxicated brother. It was a confession that Kate could not make. Not today.

"I can't explain it any better than to say that I have my reasons," she finally offered. "And it's best that Samuel not come calling or that I ride in his buggy anymore since I've vowed to help Maem and Daed with David."

Despite the fact that, clearly, Miriam was not pleased with this explanation, to Kate's relief, she asked no further questions. She did, however, point out the obvious. "Well, Samuel will be baling that hay this week," she said as she stood up and walked toward the door. "You can't be avoiding him, Kate."

"I'm not avoiding him," Kate responded, although she didn't know how true that was.

Miriam gave her a concerned look before she opened the door and disappeared into the hallway. Kate listened to the sound of her sister's bare feet on the wooden stairs as she descended to the kitchen. The third step creaked and Kate leaned back into her pillow, shutting her eyes once again.

On Wednesday, Kate had the opportunity to prove to Miriam the very words she spoke on Sunday regarding not avoiding Samuel. With rain in the forecast for Friday, Daed did not want to wait until Thursday to bale the hay. She awoke that morning knowing that Samuel would most certainly be there all day. She dreaded his presence, viewing it as a reminder of the pain she still felt over the way he had learned the truth about her sins.

If she expected him to act forlorn or avoid her, she was immediately surprised. While he seemed a bit reserved and less jovial than usual, he greeted her pleasantly as usual, then immediately focused on his work. Having helped his own *daed* with the baling of hay for many years, he didn't need instruction to know how to work the baler. Kate followed his direction, helping to stack the bales on the back of the wagon.

Daed drove the mules, four of them pulling the red baler. Samuel rode on the wagon, grabbing the bales as they emerged from the machinery. It was Kate's job to take them and stack them at the end of the long, flat wagon bed. When the stack grew too high for Kate to reach, Samuel indicated that she should sit on top, and he began tossing her the bales.

At one point she thought she saw him smile at her, and when she reached up her hand, she realized that pieces of hay were caught in the bandanna that covered her head. Embarrassed, she plucked them out and dropped them over the side of the wagon.

By the end of the morning, the one hayfield was finished and they were ready to start on the back field.

"Best be stopping for dinner, I reckon," Daed said as he stood by the wagon, his straw hat in one hand as he wiped the sweat from his brow with the other. "We'll need to unload this before we start on the back field."

Samuel peered at the sun. The still air and bright sun made it feel ten degrees hotter than it really was. His shirt was soaked with sweat, his hair matted to his head. But he had not slowed down once during the morning. "I can unload them during dinner," he said. "Will make it faster for the afternoon, *ja?*"

Daed started to argue but thought twice about it. Kate wondered if he, too, was considering the fact that Samuel might not want to share a meal with David after the outburst the previous weekend. Truth be told, she didn't blame him. Many evenings, Kate wished that she, too, could be excused from sitting at the table with him. Her disappointment in her brother was countered only by the disappointment she felt in herself.

To her astonishment, Daed motioned toward her as he responded to Samuel's offer. "She can help," he said. "Never eats much anyway. Plus, I'll have one of the girls bring out a plate for both of you."

Samuel glanced at her. "You up for that, Kate?"

His question surprised her. Why would he ask her that question? "*Ja*, of course," she heard herself say, lowering her eyes.

It was one thing to work alongside Samuel with Daed nearby. Now, however, she would be forced to work with him alone in the upper level of the barn while they unloaded the wagon. Given the amount of hay, she knew it would take about forty minutes, just enough time for Daed to enjoy his noon meal.

At first, they worked in silence. Samuel helped her, tossing the bales from the top of the wagon to the floor of the barn. Then, he jumped down and began stacking the bales. He made certain to keep the new pile separate from the old bales of hay, which, like any good farmer, Samuel surely knew Daed would want to use first, depleting his old inventory of hay before he started using the new.

As the stacks of hay grew higher, Kate tried to help him lift the bales. With hay in her dress and hair, she sneezed twice, the dust particles tickling her nose.

"God bless," he mumbled as he shoved a bale on top of the stacked hay.

She started to thank him but sneezed once again, this time taking a step backward in the process and tumbling over two bales of hay behind her. She fell down, landing in a pile of loose straw, a bewildered and embarrassed look on her face.

At this, he could no longer contain himself, and laughed loud and long.

Scrambling to her feet, she gave him an indignant look as she brushed the hay and dust from her dress. "I'm not certain what could possibly be humorous about that!"

He jumped down from the haystack and helped brush the hay from her clothing. When he finished, he stood before her, meeting her gaze, his eyes jovial instead of sorrowful. "Kate Zook! You have some explaining to do."

"I do?"

He nodded. "*Ja*, indeed. And not about falling, if that's what you are thinking."

"Then about what, Samuel?"

He took her hand in his and led her over to the side of the wagon. Without asking permission, he placed his hands on her waist and lifted her so that she could sit on the edge. He glanced over her shoulder as if to make certain that no one was coming. Clearly, he didn't want to be interrupted.

Standing before her, he crossed his arms over his chest, quietly assessing her for a few long, drawn-out seconds. Finally, he cleared his throat and started to speak. "I stopped by last Sunday to pick you up for the singing," he said.

She started to respond, but he held up his hand, stopping her before she could speak.

"Let me finish, Kate," he commanded. "I understand why you didn't want to go out that one Sunday. Your *bruder* David is a hurtful young man." The way that Samuel said that, Kate could sense his outrage over what had happened. "But why wouldn't you go with me? I'd like to know your reasoning."

When he stopped talking, she realized that he was waiting for her response.

"I told you, Samuel," she said, afraid to meet his steady gaze. "I told you that it wouldn't do you any good to be courting someone like me."

"Ah!" He uncrossed his arms and lifted a finger in the air. "That is where the explanation is needed. I want to understand this better, Kate. I want to understand what exactly you mean." He placed his hands on either side of her and peered into her face. "What does that mean? Someone like you?"

Pressing her lips together, she frowned. Was he really going to make her rehash this once again? "I'm a sinner, Samuel. Pure and simple. A sinner."

Immediately, he sobered, realizing the seriousness in her voice. "You said that the other night." He paused and tilted his head. "So you are a sinner?"

"I am," she admitted.

"And this sin is so great that even God cannot forgive you?"

"Scripture says so."

"It does?" He looked genuinely surprised. "What was this sin, Kate? If my future is to be determined by your resolve that you have such a great sin that even God would not forgive it, I believe I have the right to know what it is."

She took a deep breath and held it for a few seconds. In her mind, the words came easy. She thought them over and over again for months on end. Now, for the first time, she was to confess them out loud. She knew that, most likely, it would not be the last time.

"Samuel, I did not do the right thing." She waited for his response. There was none. "And . . . and by not doing so, I ruined two lives."

He frowned, seeming to contemplate her words. "I knew David drank alcohol," she whispered. "I even knew he was drinking that night of the accident. I refused to ride in the buggy with him. We even argued about it." She paused. "It was snowing."

Samuel nodded. "I remember."

Kate felt encouraged to continue. "I could smell it on him. Whiskey. And I told him that I wouldn't get in the buggy with him.

I'd rather walk home . . . alone and in the snow than ride with a drunk."

The memory of David's drunken arrival that night remained as fresh to her as did the image of the broken bodies in the wrecked buggy.

Samuel continued looking into her eyes.

"I saw Ruth in the buggy." She felt the tears spill from her eyes. "I had the opportunity to warn her, to tell her that he wasn't right in the head. But I didn't. Just like I never told Daed about his drinking." She cried freely, her hands covering her face. "Then I found them. I was the first person to happen upon the accident. I saw that she was dead and thought David might die, too. I raced home and woke up my parents. It was my punishment for having kept the secret."

She saw his chest rise and fall, a heavy sigh escaping through his parted lips. He moved his head and looked at her, considering her with those blue eyes that, for once, lacked joy.

"I should have warned her. I didn't do the right thing, Samuel." She wiped at her eyes with her fingertips, wishing that she had a handkerchief in her pocket. "Don't you know that God is with those who do what is right?" She lowered her eyes, too ashamed to look at Samuel as she confessed what was on her mind. "I didn't warn anyone, Samuel. I didn't do what was right."

She felt a tightness in her chest and tears in her eyes. She worried about his reaction; he was too quiet. "And then there was Jacob."

"Jacob?"

She nodded her head, gulping air to force away the sob that crept into her throat. "I was tending our farm stand by the road for Maem and watching David and Jacob. I sent Jacob and David across the road to play in the big field. I should have been watching them; they were so small."

"What happened, Kate?"

The memory remained fresh, the two little boys racing across the field, David beating Jacob by a long shot. Kate had been at the stand, rearranging the baked goods on the shelf when she saw them and called out for them to stop and wait. In hindsight, she knew she should have immediately crossed the street to get them. She didn't. And David didn't stop as she instructed. Instead, he ran across the road, laughing about having beat Jacob.

Kate looked up just as the car hit him. The woman had been on her cell phone, not paying attention. Jacob had wanted to catch up to David and wasn't old enough to know to look for cars before running into the road. It was an accident that had cost Jacob his life and nearly destroyed the family.

When the paramedics finally arrived, his small hand still clutched the roots of the black-eyed Susans and wild mint that he had collected for his *maem*.

"I . . . I should have never sent them to play in the field," Kate whispered. "Or I should have fetched them. I didn't, and he was killed. It was my fault, Samuel." The tears began to fall down her cheeks and she did nothing to stop them. "My fault that Jacob was killed and my fault that David is crippled. I could have stopped both of those accidents."

"Kate," Samuel began. "I never knew . . ."

She nodded her head. "No one knew, Samuel. I confessed my sins to the bishop before my baptism, but I reckon I have more to confess. My sins are too deep for someone as good as you. And for that reason," she choked back a sob, "I dare not go riding with you anymore."

"Is that what you think, Kate Zook?" Rather than reject her, he reached out and touched her chin with one finger, tilting her head so that she had no choice but to look at him. "That you did not do what is right and, therefore, God is no longer with you?"

With confidence, she nodded. "I don't think it. I know it." How could she explain to him that, despite knowing that God forgave all sins, it was she who found it hard to accept the proffered forgiveness? *"Therefore to him that knoweth to do good, and doeth it not, to him it is sin."*

He seemed to consider what she said, reflecting on the Bible verse for a moment. Then, without warning, he dropped his hands and took a step backward, giving her space as he nodded his head. "I see," was all he said. His eyes flickered over her shoulder once again, this time focusing on something that she could not see. Within minutes, she realized it was her *daed* and Miriam.

"Well," Samuel said. "We still have some stacking to do, then. Best get to it and we can continue this conversation later, I reckon." He reached for her hand to help her get down from the back of the wagon, but once she was on the ground, he turned back to his work, the discussion over. Samuel returned his concentration to work, and away from her.

The conversation, however, was never rekindled. Instead, Miriam and Daed helped to unload and stack the rest of the hay while Samuel and Kate picked at the food on the plate prepared by Maem. As usual, Kate had no appetite but, to her astonishment, Samuel seemed unaffected by their exchange.

CHAPTER SEVENTEEN

After two days of rain, Kate was relieved to see the sun beginning to rise on Sunday morning when she awoke. The growing fields glistened with sunlight reflecting off the raindrops that lingered on the plants. While she knew that rain made the crops and flowers grow, it had done nothing to improve her mood. She hoped that a day of sunshine might improve her state of mind.

"Hurry up, girls!" Maem called from the bottom of the stairs.

Becca struggled to put on her cape and apron while Kate pinned a black heart-shaped head covering over her bun. When she centered it on her head, Kate turned her attention to Becca. Patiently, she knelt down and straightened her sister's apron properly.

"There you go," she said.

"*Danke*, Kate," Becca mumbled. "Never will figure that out!"

Kate patted her arm as if to reassure her.

Worship service was being held down the road at the Millers' house. While not a farm, the property did have a large outbuilding that John Miller used for carpentry. Once a year, when it was their time to host the worship service, the Millers cleaned out the workroom on the second floor, sweeping all of the sawdust and removing all of the tools so that service could be held there. With big windows that looked out over the neighbor's fields of corn, it was a pleasant place to honor God.

Today, Maem accompanied her three daughters to worship. Since the service was being held so close to home, they walked instead of taking the horse and buggy. Kate walked beside her *maem*, neither one talking during the fifteen-minute walk. Becca, however, lagged behind, tugging at her white apron and grumbling about how the cape itched the back of her neck.

Even with the windows open in the room, the air felt stuffy and warm to Kate. On several occasions during the worship service, she felt her eyelids grow heavy as she listened to the deacon's words. She could hardly wait until the service ended, wanting to slip outside to get some fresh air before it was time for the fellowship meal.

After the final silent prayer, the bishop stood before the *g'may* and cleared his throat. "I must now ask for a *sitz g'may*," he said.

Kate glanced at Verna who looked as surprised as she was. A members' meeting was often called to discuss matters of importance among the church district. They were usually planned in advance. This one, however, appeared to take everyone by surprise.

The bishop waited until the nonmembers left the room, the younger children being led into a side room by the older, unbaptized girls while the boys went outside to wait in the sunshine until the conclusion of the meeting. Kate sat on the bench next to Verna and stared at the floor, wondering what needed to be discussed. She knew of no one in the hospital needing financial support or any rules that needed adjusting. *Why hadn't the bishop told the community about this meeting?* she wondered.

"We have a matter to discuss today regarding a confession," the bishop began. Immediately, Kate looked up and paid attention. Public confessions were not that common, and she wondered what on earth had happened to warrant such a display of remorse from someone in the *g'may*.

She noticed a few heads turn as if looking around the room to identify the person in question. Clearly, other people were as curious as she was.

"Samuel Esh," the bishop called out. "Please step forward."

Kate felt Verna grab her hand. Kate, however, couldn't keep her eyes off his rising figure as he stood from where he sat and walked to the front of the meeting room. Her heart pounded and her blood raced. Samuel had something to confess? In public? Her mind could think of only one thing and, in that brief moment, she felt faint at the thought.

The bishop said something to Samuel that she couldn't hear. Samuel, however, dropped to his knees and lowered his head.

"Samuel came to me, begging to be heard on a matter that is most disturbing."

Kate shut her eyes, wishing that she could stand and leave. The last thing she wanted to hear was anything that Samuel would say. A kneeling confession? She didn't want to imagine what he might confess. She only knew one thing: surely it had to do with the abrupt ending of his courtship with Ella. She only hoped it had nothing to do with Ella's unexpected and extended trip to Ohio.

"Samuel, please confess your sin to the members of our church," the bishop instructed.

Opening her eyes, Kate willed herself to stare straight ahead, despite her desire to glance in the direction of Ella Riehl's *maem* who sat on a bench two rows in front of her. She also fought the urge to look at Samuel. She could not, however, help but hear his words, despite the fact that his voice was low as he began to speak.

In the silence of the room, Samuel's words rang loud and clear. "I am a sinner," he began, his voice heavy with emotion. Whatever he had to confess, Kate knew that he must have been struggling. "I have broken the Great Commandment."

At his announcement, Kate blinked her eyes, repeating the words he had spoken in her head as if she hadn't heard him properly. *The Great Commandment?* She felt Verna loosen the hold on her hand as if she, too, were perplexed.

The bishop took a deep breath, his hands behind his back as he stared over Samuel's head at the back wall. The blank expression on his weathered face indicated that Samuel had already confessed in private to him. Certainly, whatever Samuel had done must have been very grave for the bishop to require a kneeling confession. "As is proper during a confession, I ask that you explain your sin."

Samuel hesitated. Kate couldn't stop herself from staring at him, wondering what would come from his mouth. How could Samuel have broken the Great Commandment? Had he betrayed his love for God or neighbor? She couldn't imagine that he would have done either one.

"I want to confess that I have failed to follow not just our ordinances but God's Word," he started. "I wish to make right with my sins so that I may continue serving God and our church." A soft murmur fluttered through the crowd, more people looking at one another, questioning the person seated next to them with raised eyebrows and confused expressions on their faces.

Kate felt the heat rise to her cheeks. While she knew that the confession could not be about her, her fear was that others might think it was. After all, surely he was to confess to something of an intimate nature with Ella. Since they had not courted for a while, it would be only logical for people to suspect his confession involved Kate. With dread, she waited as the bishop prodded Samuel to continue.

"A member of our *g'may* was in need and, even though I knew it, I did not extend a neighborly hand to assist," he finally said.

The bishop nodded his head, a stern look on his face as he listened to Samuel's words. "Why not, Samuel?"

"I . . . I wanted to help this person," he admitted, his eyes still downcast and staring at the floor. "Instead, I allowed myself to be swayed into inaction and neglect by listening to another person."

The bishop reached up and pulled at his white beard. He tended to do that when he was deep in thought, reflecting on what people said.

Samuel continued talking. "I looked the other way and remained silent rather than doing the right thing."

When he said that, Kate suddenly sat up straighter on the bench. Had he just said that he didn't do the right thing? She leaned forward as if trying to better hear his words.

"And did this happen just once, Samuel?"

"*Nee*," he responded. "More than once."

The murmur in the room grew louder now.

"When did this happen?"

"Months ago," he said, and then paused. Samuel moistened his lips and took a deep breath. "I witnessed a young man from our community when he was intoxicated and said nothing. He was not baptized, and I did not extend my hand to him for that reason." Kate's eyes widened as she listened to Samuel speak. Surely he was talking about David! Stunned by this admission, she stared at Samuel, even though he could not see her. "On multiple occasions, I saw this man drinking alcohol."

The bishop contemplated this and paced before Samuel. "Is there more?"

"*Ja*," Samuel responded. "One night, I saw that he was intoxicated when he arrived to pick up his *schwester*." Kate caught her breath. "When she confronted him, he fought with her. I could have intervened." He paused. "I did not, however."

"And what happened?" the bishop prodded.

"There was an accident. The man was injured, his companion killed."

"And the *schwester*?"

Samuel swallowed. "She walked home . . . in the snow . . . and found the accident scene." A few heads turned to look at Kate and she felt the color drain from her face. "I wanted to offer her a ride home, but I allowed myself to be talked out of it." He lifted his head and stared at the bishop. "I'll never know if my decision not to intervene could have saved Ruth Stoker's life or prevented David Zook's injury. But I do know that, by not stepping forward, another person has borne the brunt of guilt needlessly since the accident last December."

The members of the *g'may* began to murmur louder, their eyes traveling not just to the Stoker family but also to the Zooks. Kate didn't need to see her *maem*'s face to know that she, too, was pale. Daed had stayed home with David, so Maem faced the scrutiny on her own.

The bishop nodded his head. "You understand that Jesus commanded us to love one another as He loved us. He shared the parable of the Good Samaritan with his disciples and followers to demonstrate the love of God for His people, a love that Jesus commanded we follow: *'A new commandment I give unto you, That ye love one another; as I have loved you, that ye also love one another. By this shall all* men *know that ye are my disciples, if ye have love one to another.'* Ministering to each other in a time of need is one way to follow this commandment that Jesus gave to us. Extending a hand to help others is another way."

The bishop paused, reaching for a glass of water that rested on the windowsill. Everyone watched as he took a sip, his eyes flickering over the congregation, before he set the glass back in the same place and returned his attention to Samuel. There was no noise or movement in the room as they waited to hear what the bishop would say next.

"You also understand that God loves us and forgives us our sins, *ja?*"

Samuel nodded, the despondent look on his face indicating how strongly he felt about his sin.

The bishop exhaled and gestured with his hand so that Samuel arose from where he knelt. "I will ask that you leave the room to allow the rest of the members to discuss the matter further."

As Samuel started to turn and walk toward the exit, from the back of the room, another young man stood up. Kate leaned to the side, trying to see who it was. To her amazement, she saw Isaac. He hung his head, staring at the floor as he faced the front of the room.

"Bishop," he said, his voice catching the attention of those in the room who had not seen him stand. "If Samuel is to leave to receive punishment by the *g'may*, I shall go with him, for I, too, knew about David's drinking of alcohol." Isaac looked up, his face white and worried. "I . . . I never once thought to speak to him of his sins. Mayhaps, if I had, I could have prevented the accident."

Kate gasped, lifting her hand to cover her mouth. Another flurry of murmurs arose from the seated members.

To her surprise, there was movement on the women's side of the room. Kate's eyes widened as she saw an older woman, Martha Stoker, stand up. Ruth's *maem*. Kate felt her blood rush to her head, wondering what Martha had to say. Surely she would express her disappointment in Samuel and Isaac. Surely she would mention her heartache over the death of her dear *dochder*. Surely she would offer them forgiveness.

To Kate's surprise, just as Samuel and Isaac had done, she, too, lowered her head. "Bishop," she started, her words shaky and strained. Kate knew that she fought tears in her eyes by the sound of her voice. "I listen to these young men confessing their sins and it causes me great apprehension." Kate shut her eyes and stared at the floor, her heart breaking for Ruth's *maem*. But Martha's next words stunned her. "I, too, must confess."

At these words, Kate immediately opened her eyes and stared at the back of Martha Stoker, seeing the hunched-over shoulders and realizing that it was not from age but from angst. "I knew that my Ruth was running with David and that they were drinking that alcohol. She came home intoxicated one night. I said nothing, Bishop." She paused. "If anyone should feel guilt, it is me. I, and I alone, could have saved my *dochder's* life. But it was God's will that she was taken from us so soon."

The bishop looked bewildered, staring at the three people before him. The rest of the members were openly mumbling, breaking the stunned silence that had previously held sway.

And then, one more person stood.

Kate squeezed Verna's hand. A hush fell throughout the room as Maem stood up, facing the bishop in silence for a few long, drawn-out moments. Kate wondered what Maem would say, worried that the pain of what had just been said about her son would break her *maem* at last. Indeed, as Maem stood there, the eyes of the other members upon her, she wrung her hands and bowed her head before she took a deep breath and finally spoke.

"I, too, Bishop, must confess."

Catching her breath, Kate's eyes darted over the heads of the women seated before her to look to where Samuel stood. He remained still, his eyes downcast. She wished that he would look at her. Even more importantly, she wished that she understood why he had done this.

"When my son Jacob died," Maem continued, "I . . . I didn't accept God's will. I questioned His reasons for taking Jacob." Jacob? At the mention of her deceased brother, Kate returned her gaze to her *maem's* back, her heart aching for the pain she knew Maem must surely feel. *How does Jacob play into this?* she wondered.

"Rather than deal with my grief," Maem said, her voice quiet and barely audible. "I . . . I hid in my root garden, nurturing the last gift my son gave to me. Rather than admit my own fault at not being there to watch the *kinner* that day, and leaving an eight-year-old in charge of their care, I permitted my son David to harbor ill will toward his *schwester* over Jacob's death. When David began to drink, he did so continue without either of his parents addressing the problem."

Fighting the urge to gasp at her *maem*'s words, Kate pressed her lips together and swallowed. Her parents knew? Maem blamed herself for Jacob's death? The revelation left her breathless and, for just a moment, Kate felt as if a weight had been lifted from her shoulders.

But Maem wasn't finished. She choked back a sob. "After the accident, I realized alcohol was involved. His *daed* found a whiskey bottle in the wrecked buggy and asked me to discard it so that the Englische authorities would not know."

The bishop gestured to Samuel to remain standing, rather than leave the room. Kate saw his chest rise as he inhaled, breathing deeply as he contemplated the scene unfolding before him. He stared at the people who stood before him, the expression in his face softening as he did so.

"No matter what we feel or think, we must remember that denying another person help is indeed wrong. However, it does not negate the fact of the original transgression." He gestured for everyone to sit down in their seats. Kate watched as Samuel made his way back to his place among the young unmarried men. He continued to stare straight ahead, never once looking in her direction.

"We are all sinners," the bishop said, his eyes scanning the room. "That is why God sent His son to save us." He nodded his head at Samuel. "Samuel Esh has spoken of his sins. In doing so, it is apparent that many others, perhaps even some who have not spoken up, made the same error of judgment in a similar situation. But we must remember one thing . . ." He glanced around the room again, this time letting his eyes rest on Kate. "God forgives even the worst sinner," he said at last. "All we have to do is ask."

He motioned again toward Samuel. "I commend you, Samuel Esh, for feeling so strongly about this as to request a public confession before the *g'may*."

Kate's head snapped in Samuel's direction. He had requested that he be allowed to confess in public? Emotions welled in her throat as she began to realize what had not been said: that he'd confessed on purpose in order to let her know she was not alone in how she felt.

"Oh help," she whispered. She reached again for Verna's hand.

"But the guilt you have borne has surely been punishment enough," the bishop said. Then, as if in an afterthought, he added, "For all of you who knew of this sin and felt guilt. I want to remind everyone of Proverbs 3, verses 5 and 6: *'Trust in the Lord with all your heart, and do not lean on your own understanding. In all your ways acknowledge him, and he will make straight your paths.'* It is not up to us to question the decisions that He makes, as long as we accept the Lord and love Him, regardless of the situation and the outcome. *'He will make straight your paths.'"*

CHAPTER EIGHTEEN

She sat on the porch, gently rocking back and forth in the shade from the overhang. She rested her head on the back of the rocking chair, watching as the sun set in the sky. The colors shifted, changing from oranges and reds to purples and blues. Occasionally a bird would fly by, chirping a good-night song as it dipped down through the growing cornfields.

What a long and unusual day, she thought. While she didn't profess to understand her feelings about everything that had happened, she did sense a release of tension at home. Upon returning from worship service, Maem sought out Daed. They disappeared outside for a while and Kate suspected that she was sharing the events of the members' meeting. Since Miriam and Becca were not baptized yet, they did not know what had occurred. However, Kate was certain they suspected something important happened, especially when Maem didn't stay for fellowship but left shortly after the service.

After she had returned home, Kate found her *maem* kneeling in her herb garden. Cautiously, Kate slipped through the wooden gate and approached her. For a few long minutes, Kate stood behind her *maem*, watching in silence as she prayed.

"Sometimes I feel him here."

The words had been so soft that Kate almost didn't hear them.

"Who, Maem?"

"Jacob."

Kate didn't speak.

"I shut my eyes and I see him," she continued. "I can even hear his laugh." A soft chuckle slipped through her lips. "I spent so much time lamenting the past that I reckon I forgot how to live in the present."

Kate knew what she meant. She, too, had done the same thing . . . until Samuel had forced her to begin living again.

"I'm so sorry, Kate." Maem glanced over her shoulder. "I never meant to burden you with guilt. It wasn't fair."

Taking a step forward, Kate placed her hand on Maem's shoulder, a gesture of both understanding and forgiveness. Maem tilted her head, pressing her cheek against the back of Kate's hand. For a long while, they stood like that, mother and daughter, sharing a moment of silence that spoke louder than words.

Now, as she sat on the porch, Kate sighed and shut her eyes for a moment, trying to wrap her head around what all had occurred that day.

Oh, she had suspected that Daed knew about the whiskey bottle in the buggy. She never once thought that Maem was aware of it. From the sounds of it, however, neither of her parents had been oblivious to David's inclination to drink alcohol. They had also been aware it had caused the accident.

And for all of these months, Kate had thought she was the only one, and had blamed herself thoroughly. Now it was clear that other members of the *g'may* had also witnessed and knew of David's problematic behavior. She realized that she needed to rethink the events of the past six months.

When Maem and Daed returned inside the house, they seemed to watch Kate with great apprehension. With Miriam, Becca, and David around, Kate knew that they would not say anything to her. But she was curious as to what they had discussed. For some reason, they seemed stronger and more unified, not responding to David right away when he demanded a glass of water or a blanket. Kate imagined that he, too, suspected something was amiss. For once, his bark had a little less bite.

She couldn't say that she was displeased.

Her thoughts were interrupted by the sound of a horse and buggy driving down the lane. Her pulse quickened: Samuel.

She sat up, her feet on the porch to steady the rocking chair as she waited for him to park the buggy and walk toward the porch. He still wore his Sunday clothes, his black hat perched atop his head, slightly tilted so that his eyes were shaded from the sun.

"Hello there, Kate Zook," he said as he put one foot on the porch step but remained standing on the walkway.

She forced a small smile, feeling awkward after the dramatic incident at the members' meeting earlier that day. "Hello, Samuel," she managed to reply. Out of the corner of her eye, she saw movement at the window. Maem peered out, but upon seeing Samuel standing there with Kate, she backed away. Kate suspected that no one would disturb them.

He glanced up at the sky, squinting as he did so. "Nice day out, *ja*?"

She exhaled. "I reckon you didn't come here to give me a weather report."

He pursed his lips as he looked back at her, contemplating his response. Deciding against trying to counter her statement, he shook his head. "*Nee*, Kate," he admitted. "I did not." He pushed his hands into his front pockets and stood up straight. "I came to see if you might take a little ride with me." He glanced at the buggy as if she didn't fully understand what he meant. "To talk a spell."

For a moment, she thought she might decline. After all, no one would bother them on the porch. She felt drained, emotionally and spiritually, and didn't want to go out. But by nature, she tried not to be difficult. So she nodded her head and stood up, smoothing down the front of her dress before she followed him down the walkway toward his buggy.

He waited to speak until they were on the main road, heading away from her parents' farm. The air felt warm, even in the open buggy. Thankfully, he drove toward the east so that the sun was not beating on their faces.

"You left worship right after the meeting," he said.

She shrugged. There wasn't much to say in way of response. However, she didn't want to be construed as rude. "I suspect Maem didn't feel so well afterwards."

He nodded his head as if he understood what she was saying.

They rode in silence, the horse's hooves clacking against the road and the wheels of the buggy making a gentle whirling sound. Kate listened to the noise, relaxing under its musical cadence.

"Why'd you do it, Samuel?"

Her question surprised both of them. She had been thinking those words and almost didn't believe she spoke them aloud until she realized that he was clearing his throat to answer.

"*Vell*, Kate," he started slowly. "You said something the other day, when we were talking in the hay barn. You said that if a person knows something is wrong and does no good that it's a sin. You said that God was no longer with you. I pondered that, Kate. And do you know what I realized?" He paused but didn't wait for an answer. "If God was no longer with you, then I reckoned God was no longer with me, either."

"I . . . I don't understand . . ." The words trailed off, Kate unable to put into words the thought that crossed her mind.

"Oh, Kate," he said, pulling the buggy over to the side of the road. He held the reins in one hand and turned toward her. "Did you really think that you alone bore the burden of knowing David's secret? Did you truly believe that you could have stopped him?"

She blinked, but remained silent.

"Many of us knew that he drank. I reckon any one of our youth members could have stood and confessed today that they, too, could have spoken up! Why, any one of us could have confronted him."

Many? This shocked her. Was he saying that even more people who'd confessed at the meeting knew about David's sinful drinking? In the months following the accident, no one had spoken about the real cause. Instead, they'd focused on mourning Ruth's death and praying for David's healing. Only Kate had dwelled upon the fact that an empty whiskey bottle lay broken under the wreckage. But maybe others had as well, she realized now.

"Why, one time I saw him leaving that store on the main thoroughfare," he continued. "You know, the place that sells liquor and doesn't pay attention to whether the person is underage or Amish? I knew what David carried in that brown paper bag."

"Did he see you?"

Samuel nodded. "*Ja*, he did indeed. He just grinned and waved, Kate, as if it was the most natural thing for a seventeen-year-old Amish boy to buy whiskey."

Stunned, Kate turned her back toward Samuel. She needed time to think about this revelation. For months she had wallowed in the guilt of covering up for her brother's addiction. Oh, she'd confronted David on more than one occasion before the accident, but his defense that he was merely enjoying his *rumschpringe* had swayed her to remain silent. After all, he always pointed out, he hadn't taken the kneeling vow yet.

Still, the memory of that night . . . the way she had let him walk away, knowing Ruth was in the buggy. That decision had haunted her. It burned inside of her for months, the guilt making her unable to forgive herself. It had been sinful to avoid the confrontation.

And she had sinned in similar ways other times. How many times had she covered for him, not informing her *daed* that David had been drinking at the social gatherings? She dare not even attempt to count them! And all along, she thought that his secret remained with her and her alone.

"I never knew that anyone else was aware . . ."

Samuel placed his hand on her arm. "Kate," he said. "You cannot claim the responsibility for the sins of your *bruder*." He contemplated something, as if he had more to say to her.

"What is it, Samuel?"

"I need to confess something more to you," he said. He looked uncomfortable, the muscles in his jaw twitching. "Mayhaps this will help to explain a few things."

Once again, her curiosity piqued, she waited for him to speak.

"I knew that David drank alcohol that evening," he admitted. "In fact, I was there that night of the accident. You know, at the singing. I stood at the door, waiting for Ella to fetch her shawl, when I overheard you arguing with David outside the door."

He gave her a moment to digest what he had just said. Kate searched her memory, wondering if this were true. And then she remembered sensing a presence on the porch as she'd faced off with David—how that person had held up a light that had illuminated his twisted, angry expression. She nearly gasped in surprise. A person had seen their exchange. And that person had been Samuel.

"I didn't know . . ." she said, trailing off.

Samuel reached out to take her hand and, ever so lightly, held it in his hand. Gently, he caressed her skin with his thumb. "Kate,

I wanted to step forward and confront David that night, perhaps even drive the buggy home for him, but . . .”

He didn't need to finish that thought for they both knew that he had not done so.

“And then, when he left and I saw you standing there, the snow on your bonnet and cape, I wanted to offer you a ride.”

Kate raised an eyebrow at this admission. “Why didn't you?”

He shook his head and sighed, a look of regret on his face. “Believe me, Kate, I asked myself that same question every day for weeks after the accident.” He paused, looking away for a moment. Kate waited for him to collect his thoughts. Clearly, this confession was difficult for him. She could see how he struggled to find the proper words to convey his feelings. “If I had driven up that road to take you home, mayhaps we could have saved Ruth. Better yet, mayhaps it could have been avoided.”

“So what happened?” she asked, almost afraid to hear the answer.

“I told you once about a disagreement I had with someone about doing a good thing. Do you remember?” He removed his hat and set it between them on the buggy seat, shifting his weight in the seat so that he was turned toward her. “I had already asked Ella to ride home. When I suggested that we take you home, she wasn't partial to the idea of you joining us. For that reason, I did not extend the invitation but, instead, let you walk home alone . . . in the snow.”

He let his hand fall from her shoulder and took her hand in his. “Kate, that decision haunted me. When I heard what happened, I knew that had I listened to my instinct, had *I* done the right thing, I might have saved you from finding the accident scene.” He chewed on his lower lip, thinking for a moment before he continued. “Even worse, I realized that I had allowed myself to be persuaded from doing the right thing by Ella. For all of her godly traits and righteousness, her lack of compassion toward you in a time of need was something that stuck with me. It made me realize that she was not the woman for me."

Kate gave a soft gasp, trying to understand what he meant. Did Ella realize this episode was the reason Samuel quit her? If so, suddenly it became clear why Ella blamed Kate for Samuel ending their courtship.

"After I visited with David, I saw what you were living with, Kate." The muscles in his jaw tensed as he remembered David's harsh treatment. "I felt angry, Kate. I realized that he blamed you for his situation rather than accepting responsibility for it. He avoided admitting the truth and took his aggression out on you."

"He's suffering . . ." she started to say, but Samuel held up his hand to stop her in midsentence.

"Kate, no one deserves to be talked to in such a manner." A look of contempt flashed across his face as he remembered. "After that Sunday supper, I harbored a lot of anger toward David and I had to pray to release it. After all, he, too, is my neighbor."

She understood what he meant. Even the hurt and forlorn need prayers and love. That was what God wanted from His people. It was one of the main reasons why she tolerated David's cruelty.

"But even though he needs consideration and forgiveness, he also needs to learn to accept God's will and adapt," Samuel added. "Not to blame others. To do so is to put himself in God's place."

She hadn't considered that perspective before and tilted her head, digesting his words. Had David been playing God with her life? With the lives of her entire family?

Samuel seemed to read her thoughts. "I began to realize how his manipulation was affecting you and how you felt you must make such a sacrifice. You asked why I confessed today. Kate, I could no longer remain silent about what I knew and how I had contributed to the situation.

"You must know, Kate, that it was no coincidence that I happened to be driving along your road on that Saturday when you were walking home from Susan's."

Her eyes grew wide as she silently questioned him.

"Did you not hear what I said the other day? About my future? I want my future to include you, Kate Zook. Any woman who could stand up for her values and beliefs, who faced such devastation with such honor and dignity . . . well, I knew that was the woman for me."

"I . . . I don't understand . . ."

"What I am saying, Kate Zook, is that I want you to be Samuel's Kate, my *fraa*. I want you to plant celery in your garden and, come October, marry me."

"Oh!"

"I just pray that I can prove myself as virtuous and righteous as you have shown yourself to be," he added.

She scarcely believed what she heard. After confessing her deepest sins to Samuel, not only had he admitted his own sin but he praised her? "I would never consider myself those things, Samuel," she whispered. "If you think so, you will surely be disappointed."

He lifted her hand to his mouth, pausing before gently brushing his lips against her skin. "*Nee*, Kate," he replied. "I have seen you stand up against Satan, and even when Satan thought he won, you proved yourself a formidable foe. You wear the armor of God wisely, Kate. Any man would be proud to call you his wife." He took a deep breath before adding, "I'd like that man to be me."

Wife. The word sounded strange as she repeated it in her head. *Wife.* All Amish girls were raised with the idea that, one day, they would marry a good Amish man and raise a family, instilling the love of God in their *kinner* so that they, too, would one day decide to become part of the Amish community. It was a cycle that had been repeating itself for hundreds of years and was the main reason that the Amish communities continued to grow.

Yet, she had all but given up on that dream, especially after David's accident. Without David's help, who would assist Daed? When her parents passed, who would take care of David?

"I . . . I don't know what to say," she stammered.

He lifted an eyebrow, his blue eyes bright as he stared at her. "I'd like to think you'd say yes."

"Oh, Samuel," she started. "Of course I'd love to say yes." The hesitation in her voice did not detract from the warm glow on his face. "But my *daed* . . ." she countered, lifting her eyes to look at Samuel. "The burden of tending the farm would fall on Miriam and Becca. I don't know if I could do that to them, Samuel."

Once again, he lifted his hand to stop her, a smile on his lips. "No burden will fall to your *schwesters*, Kate. I've already had discussions with your *daed* about that."

"Discussions?" she repeated. He had discussed this with Daed? While she was surprised to learn this, she finally felt she could make sense of recent changes in her *daed*'s demeanor. After Samuel's help following her injury, Daed had seemed unusually relaxed and cheerful. Certainly that must have been when Samuel talked with Daed. "About what?"

"*Vell*, Kate," Samuel began slowly. "Your *daed* has that *grossdaadihaus, ja*? I know it hasn't been lived in for a while, but I would fix it up for us to live there. It might be small, but it would certainly do for a few years. Then when the time is right, when Miriam and Becca are settled down, your parents can claim their life right and move there while you and I live in the main house."

A soft gasp escaped her lips. "Oh," she whispered.

"I'll work the farm alongside your *daed* and buy the farm when he is ready to sell. Besides what money I've already saved, some of my labor will go toward the purchase of the farm, of course."

That he already had a plan didn't surprise her, for she knew that the Amish always maintained honor among deals. In addition, the farm was larger than anything Samuel could have afforded otherwise. "Your *daed* was right pleased with the idea."

"But what about David . . . ?"

Samuel took a deep breath, clearly not as enthusiastic about this aspect of his plan. "Your parents have harbored guilt, Kate. Just as you have. Now that we have confessed our sins, I'm hoping that they can move past this. David, too, will need to learn that his disability does not mean that he cannot contribute to the well-being of the family."

While she'd love to believe that was possible, she held doubt that it would actually happen.

"The bishop is stopping by, too, Kate," he added, a solemn edge in his voice. "When I went to the bishop and told him what I wanted to do, I explained the reasons why. The bishop had no idea of the extent of the issues and reassured me that the matter would be addressed after the worship service. He said he would stop by this afternoon, Kate. That's one of the reasons I wanted to take you for a ride earlier than usual." He reached for her hand one more time. "That and to find out what your answer is to my proposal. I don't want to presume anything, Kate. Will you marry me in October?"

She blinked her eyes, feeling the tears welling up and threatening to spill over. For a moment, she felt as if she would wake up only to realize that this was nothing more than a dream. *How had so much happened in just a few months?* From David's accident to accepting her fate as a *maedel*, a young woman destined to never marry, to suddenly courting Samuel, everything felt surreal. Not only had the truth come out, it had set her free from the chains of self-condemnation. Now Samuel was asking for her hand.

When she realized that Samuel was still waiting for her answer, she laughed and wiped at the tears in her eyes. "Yes, Samuel," she heard herself say, a warm feeling growing in her heart. "I will most certainly marry you in October."

He grinned, reaching out to pull her into his arms. She relaxed in his embrace and felt his heart pounding against her chest. That was when she realized that, despite appearing calm and at ease, he had been nervous. Had he actually feared that she might refuse him?

With his arms around her, she felt protected and safe. She knew that there would be many challenges ahead of them, especially since they would remain on the Zook farm. However, she knew that, together, they would face the hard times and, as long as they continued to abide by their faith and honor their love for God, grace would surely follow them.

EPILOGUE

She stood at the window, her eyes scanning the grayish sky. The dark clouds and crisp air indicated the inevitability of the winter's first snow. As she stood there watching, she caught movement near the barn and turned her attention in that direction. When she realized that it was Samuel, hurrying through the shadows toward their house, she smiled and moved to the door to open it for him.

He shivered as he walked into the house, slapping at his arms to warm up. "Sure is cold out there!" With his pink cheeks and bright eyes, it was clear that he was glad his day was over.

"I have coffee ready." She helped him take off his coat and hung it on the hook by the door.

"First snow tonight, you reckon?" He set his hat on the bench by the door and sniffed at the air. "Something smells right *gut*, Kate," he said as he followed her into the kitchen.

They had moved in the previous week, just two weeks after their wedding. Everything still felt unusual and different, not just the fact that they were living in the *grossdaadihaus*, but that they were married at last.

Hurrying to the stove, Kate poured him a cup of coffee and set it on the counter before turning to the refrigerator for the milk. He washed his hands at the sink and, as he dried them on a dishtowel, leaned against the counter to watch her. She knew she was being observed, which made her feel nervous as she prepared his coffee: two sugars and a dash of milk, just the way he liked it.

"That warms up a fellow, all right!" he said as he accepted the mug. He peered at her over the rim as he sipped the coffee. "And you, Kate Esh. How was your day, my *fraa*?"

She tried not to smile at his playful tone. Over the past few weeks, she had learned a lot about her husband: the foods he liked, the way he worked, and the manner he teased. Their first weeks together had been nothing less than heaven on earth as far as Kate was concerned. His attentiveness to her, not just as his wife but also as his friend, warmed her heart each and every day.

"It was just *wunderbar*," she said. "Worked some more on my quilt. Maem came over for an hour to help."

"Wonder that she managed the long journey," he teased.

Kate laughed, especially since the main house was separated from the *grossdaadihaus* by two doors and the large gathering room used for worship service. "She's invited some of the women over for Saturday next to finish the quilting. I'm just sorry that we didn't have it ready before the wedding."

"Before or after," he said. "Doesn't much matter as long as we're warm at night." Setting down the coffee mug on the counter, he reached his hand out to take hers. "I have good news," he said as he pulled her into his arms, holding her tight as he stared down into her face. He brushed back a stray hair that had fallen from her *kapp*. "We have a breakthrough with David," he said, not able to hide the pride in his voice.

"Oh my!" Kate was genuinely curious. "Do tell!"

Samuel nodded. "*Ja*! A real breakthrough. I managed to convince him to help with the afternoon milking. He takes the milk to the refrigeration container and brings back the empty buckets.

Actually saves us some time, which, given how cold it is, was much appreciated."

"How *wunderbar!*"

Brushing his fingers along the side of her neck, Samuel studied her face. "I think those meetings he's been having with the deacon are finally helping, Kate. We may have turned a corner at last. He never complained once."

That was, indeed, good news. "Praise the Lord, Samuel."

Indeed, things seemed to be changing for the better over the past few months. For Kate, the summer months leading up to her autumn wedding had passed far too quickly. Besides her regular chores during the day, she'd kept busy spending more time with Samuel.

His presence at the Zook farm increased, particularly in the evenings and on Saturdays. Besides helping Daed with haying, he spent time working on the *grossdaadihaus*. While it didn't need major renovations, Samuel insisted that the floors be refinished, the walls repainted, and the kitchen updated with newer cabinets and appliances.

For the first few weeks after their wedding, Samuel remained at his parents' farm. The *grossdaadihaus* wasn't finished and he wanted to help his *daed* with filling the silo. On the weekends he stayed at the Zook farm so that he could help her *daed*, work on the house, and attend worship with Kate. It was customary for the newly married to not live together right away, usually not until spring. But once the *grossdaadihaus* was finished, Samuel saw no reason to delay the move to their new home.

For the first few days, Kate had felt shy and awkward, fixing Samuel a breakfast that she was used to seeing her *maem* fix for Daed and her siblings. When Samuel came home for the noon meal, she tried to have something special prepared for him but, after a few days, they both agreed that they would share the noon meal with her family next door. It was hard to cook for two people, she decided. Plus, she missed the interaction with her parents.

Pulling back, Samuel glanced around the kitchen, noticing the set table and lantern burning. With the propane heater on, the kitchen felt warm and inviting. "I smell fresh bread," he said, smiling like a mischievous boy. "I don't believe I've had the pleasure yet, Kate Esh!"

"And a snitz pie!"

Samuel looked genuinely surprised. "Snitz pie? That's my favorite."

"I know." His *maem* had shared that information with her during their visit the previous Sunday afternoon. "That's why I made it."

"And to think," he teased, "I was worried about your cooking way back when we went for that hike. Figured you had to have a flaw somewhere. With nothing else in sight, I guessed it had to be your cooking!"

She flushed. "No one is perfect, Samuel. I have plenty of flaws."

Good-naturedly, he nodded his head. "*Ja*, I know," he said. "But I'm sure glad I don't see them!"

Kate laughed and her cheeks flushed at the compliment. Samuel took his seat and looked over the table with satisfaction as steam rose from the food she'd prepared. His blue eyes met hers, and together, they bent their heads for a silent prayer.

A few minutes later, she looked up to see the first few snowflakes beginning to fall outside the window. She almost pointed this out to Samuel, but then noticed that he was already gazing at the flurries coming down. When he turned to her with a reassuring smile, she knew that despite the arrival of winter, which brought back all the memories of the previous year, she had nothing to fear. With Samuel by her side, she could finally feel safe and protected from all of life's unexpected storms.

GLOSSARY OF PENNSYLVANIA DUTCH

aendi	aunt
Ausbund	Amish hymnal
boppli	baby
bruder	brother
Daed, or her *daed*	Father
danke	thank you
Englische	non-Amish people
ferhoodled	confused/daydreaming
fraa	wife
g'may	church district
grossdaadihaus	small house attached to main house
gut	good
gut mariye	good morning
ja	yes
kapp	cap
kinner	children
kum esse	come eat
maedel	a single woman
Maem, or her *maem*	Mother
nee	no

onkel	uncle
Ordnung	unwritten rules of the *g'may*
rumschpringe	period of "fun" time for youths
schwester	sister
sitz g'may	members' meeting after worship
vorsinger	choir director
wie geht's?	what's going on?
wunderbar gut	wonderfully good

ABOUT THE AUTHOR

The Preiss family emigrated from Europe in 1705, settling in Pennsylvania as the area's first wave of Mennonite families. Sarah Price has always respected and honored her ancestors through exploration and research about her family's history and their religion. At nineteen, she befriended an Amish family and lived on their farm throughout the years.

Sarah Price splits her time between her home outside of New York City and an Amish farm in Lancaster County, Pennsylvania, where she retreats to reflect, write, and reconnect with her Amish friends and Mennonite family.

Find Sarah Price on Facebook and Goodreads! Learn about upcoming books, sequels, series, and contests. You can contact the author at sarahprice.author@gmail.com. Or visit her online at sarahpriceauthor.wordpress.com or on Facebook at www.facebook.com/fansofsarahprice.